SOUTHERN GENTLEMEN

by

Tony Burnett

Dedicated to the memory of

Howard Burnett

1920-2001

for sharing his love of words

Table of Contents

BAIT

I own four perfectly seasoned cast iron skillets, the oldest of which I've had for almost 40 years. My late mother gave it to me when I first permanently moved out of the home place during my junior year of college. It came with a complete set of kitchen ware - plates, glasses, utensils, everything. I still have the skillet.

I learned to cook by the time I was nine. I was the oldest but my brother and sister had to learn too. When we each turned twelve we became responsible for preparing the dinner meal one night a week. Both my parents liked to cook and they were good at it. They also liked to get snockered and they were good at that too. When all three siblings were teens Dad and Mom got snockered any night when there was no school function, but thanks to the kids we all ate well. I probably enjoyed cooking more than anyone in the family. It was a creative outlet and if I did the cooking I didn't have to wash dishes. I don't even like to load the dishwasher and we didn't have one.

When I was tall enough to reach the back of the stove, I received my first cooking lesson. My mom said, "The way to a man's heart is through his stomach." At the time I assumed this was some strange sort of anatomy lesson as I had just finished helping my dad butcher a dozen rabbits. He would teach me the names of the individual organs as we eviscerated the animals. Once I understood what my mom really meant I was still a bit confused. I was a boy. Did she assume that just because I didn't like sports, I was a homosexual? I didn't like sports because I was as gangly and clumsy as a day old colt, plus there were no girls. Contrary to her opinion, I did like girls, a lot. I can't remember back to a day when I was not sexually attracted to girls, women, females. I was born horny. But I digress.

Now my kitchen is a state of the art studio of cast iron, stainless steel, ceramic and glass. No aluminum or plastic will be found in my creative space. I have some of the finest quality utensils imported from around the world. "I Have a Wok and I'm Not Afraid to Use It" was the title of my first, well only, cookbook. It sold a whopping 318 copies. My publisher said I probably jumped onto the stir fry bandwagon a bit too late. I'm more inclined to think that I cook much better than I write.

As I've mentioned, I'm a big fan of women. I think the best age for women is their thirties. I started dating women in their thirties when I was seventeen. At 60, I still prefer women in their thirties. I even married one once. I was twenty-six. She was thirty-three. It lasted six years. That was my only marriage and probably my longest relationship, seeing as how we still got together fairly often for another five or six years after our divorce and her rather immediate remarriage. She said she out grew me.

"Don't worry," I told her. "I've heard that from much younger women than you." I don't think I saw her again after that. Sometimes I tend to spout off without really considering the impact of what I'm saying.

"Mouthy Bastard!" is how Jeanine described it. She was one of my "calendar girls". I call her that not because she was drop-dead gorgeous, although life is too short to hang out with ugly women.

"Calendar girl" to me means someone with who you can measure the length of your relationship on a calendar as opposed to a clock.

I like to spoil women and I'm good at it. "Extremely talented," according to Becca, another "calendar girl" who actually made it through two calendars. The downside of that is I end up with needy women who eventually either get whiny or get over it. Either way, one of us gets bored and calls it quits. That's usually just a temporary setback. I learned a valuable lesson from Mama even though I had to adjust the gender. Women love to be cooked for. They love having gourmet coffee served to them in bed. They will do almost anything for (or with) a ripe California strawberry hand dipped in dark chocolate.

"Don't you get it? There's more to life than food and sex!" That was Claire. I don't think she took more than a month out of the calendar.

"Really? What could be more important than food and sex?" There goes that mouth again. Her face turned an extreme shade of purple just before she screamed. "You know what I mean you arrogant shithead!" She slammed the door behind her before ever answering my question.

So why am I driving all over the county with my cell phone to my ear, weaving on the road and calling every pertinent number I can think of? It's Rhonda. Rhonda is not even in her thirties. She's forty four or forty five. She was already 40 when we met. She's not the same as most of the women I've known. Oh, she likes being spoiled enough but she doesn't seem to need it. She never allows any score cards in our relationship. "You do what you want. I'll do what I want. Maybe we can have some fun together."

It was four years ago she told me that and four months before she moved in. The day she moved in I made stuffed trout and creamed broccoli. She did the dishes after dinner and brought me a margarita on the rocks. She took a sip of it, sat on my lap and said "This just might work." It did work. Hell, I thought it was still working. We got up early, had breakfast together. She went to her job. I went to mine. We came home, glad to see each other, and talked about our day. We planned outings. We shopped together. We made love frequently and passionately. She even overlooked my occasional off color or thoughtless comment.

Whenever we go anywhere in the car, she drives. That's fine with me. I would rather observe the scenery. She knows the names of every other driver on the road, either "Asshole" or "Son of a Bitch", which I find entertaining. It only takes a minor infraction on another driver's part and she identifies them emphatically. I snicker under my breath and she cocks her head in my direction. "Well he is!"

A couple of weeks ago we were sitting at the table over a breakfast of migas, potatoes au gratin and toast when she put down her fork in mid meal and asked "What do you want to do with your life?"

"I'm doing it." I replied.

"No, seriously, I mean long term."

"I am serious. I'm perfectly happy. I love you." I was being honest.

"Well, I love you too but there has to be more to it, some goal."

"I'm going to retire in a few years then I can really spoil you, like a house husband."

"We would have to get married for that." She observed.

"Okay then, I'll be your concubine, your love slave."

"Can you just be serious for a minute?"

"If I do will you still love me?"

"Why don't you try me?"

"I am serious. I like things the way they are. What do we need to change?"

"I don't know, it just seems like there should be more to it."

I mentally checked the calendar. It wasn't that time of the month. Her birthday wasn't coming up. It must be something in the water. I let it pass. The next few days she seemed a little distant. I bent over backwards trying to make her comfortable. I washed her hair. I gave her massages. I prepared her favorite seafood dish. Still the cloud would not pass.

Today, when she didn't come home from work, I tried her cell phone. It's turned off. I called her office. They said she left early, something about needing to have her car looked at. She hadn't mentioned a problem with her car but as distant as she had been lately it didn't surprise me. I started looking around the house. Most of her things were here but some of her clothes, most of her makeup and a couple of suitcases were gone. I was concerned.

Now it's approaching 11pm. I'm out looking everywhere, calling all her friends. All but one knows nothing. Her friend, Joel, from work says, "You'll have to talk to her" and hangs up. That's ominous. I'm heading back to the house when the phone rings.

"Meet me at Kerbey Lane on Lamar. I have to show you something." She sounded happier and more excited than she had in weeks.

"That's twenty miles. It's almost midnight."

A long pause.

"Never mind." She now sounded dejected.

"Why don't you show me when you get home?

"I'm not coming home."

Shit! "I'll be there in half an hour." I hoped she didn't hear the exasperation in my voice.

"You don't have to come."

"Are you kidding? I love surprises!" Maybe I could bring back the lilt I heard earlier.

"Cool." The call ended.

I have two words to describe what I do when a woman goes skitsy on me. "Run away!"

This time, I let my curiosity get the better of me. Besides, I felt like what Rhonda and I had was at least worth ending face to face. Twenty five minutes later I was pulling in to the Kerbey Lane Café. The parking lot was crowded but I didn't see Rhonda's car. I decided to wait inside. As soon as I entered, I saw her at a corner table by the window. She smiled when our eyes met.

"Hungry?" She asked.

"I could eat," now that my stomach had stopped churning.

"Good, I waited to order," she said, trying to be nonchalant but I could tell she was about to pop. I wasn't going to let her off that easy.

"Where's your car? I asked.

"Right there." She pointed out the window.

"I don't see it"

"The black one," she smiled.

Just outside the window was parked one of those little two-seater convertible sports cars like guys named "Asshole" drive.

"Cute, ain't it!" She almost giggled.

"Can you afford that?" I asked, knowing full well she could.

"Gee, I hope so." She was back to her bubbliest.

"So that's what you wanted to show me?"

"Nope." Okay, now I was stunned.

"Well, what then?"

Just then the waiter came to take our order. The special looked good but for once my mind wasn't on food. "I'll have the special"

"Me too." Rhonda agreed.

"Okay," she said. "Here's the deal." She slid an envelope across the table.

"Well, these can't be divorce papers. We're not married. Are you suing me?" That mouth again. She literally growled at me but I could tell by her eyes she was playing. I opened the envelope. Inside were two round trip tickets to Milan, departing at 10 am on what was now this morning.

"I, my job, what about? - I've got to get clothes. – I don't see how? – We can't do that!"

"I brought your clothes and passport. You'll have to work out the rest." I knew what she meant by that. My stomach was churning again. Our meal came. I stared at it. Was I scared or excited? A million reasons not to go entered my mind. It was irresponsible. She was crazy. I'm too old for this shit!

"I need a shower."

"You can shower at my hotel room." She offered.

"Cool." I picked up my fork.

FAT TUESDAY

In less than a millisecond the rays emanate from the glowing pumpkin on the horizon. They pierce the atmosphere, ooze through the smog, dance off the bronze mirrored skyscrapers and slam to their death against the gray concrete three story supporting Hans and his companion. From the street below dissonant electric guitar chords tangle the various genres, volumes and keys into an aural sewage stream assaulting the ears of any music aficionado. The growing crowd of revelers down on Sixth Street don't seem to care. Instead they are gyrating as one amorphous body to a pair of barefoot street drummers pounding out aboriginal rhythms on an assortment of overturned plastic buckets. Even Hans taps his alligator boot. He can see well beyond the Capitol building to the north. His attention, however, is fixed on the street below, especially the southwest entrance to the Driskill Hotel. He lets another raw oyster slide down his throat offering the shell to his thick-jowled companion who licks the salty phlegm from the object and drops it at his feet. Hans raises two fingers and points at his table. The waitress brings another cognac. It is the Fat Tuesday celebration and he is enjoying it as best he can.

Six years as roommates has all but eliminated the language barrier between Hans and Artemis. As Hans strokes his friend's forehead, Artemis turns his eyes imploringly toward Hans and licks his massive chops asking for another oyster shell. The bulldog's request is granted.

"It's almost time," Hans says to Artemis. Together they stare toward the entrance to the Driskill. Hans checks his Rolex. At exactly 6:08 pm she emerges. It is not so much her stunning beauty that draws his attention but that she is so misplaced. She walks erectly, dressed in a starched white blouse and tan mid-length skirt, her blonde hair pulled behind her ears with a white band. Beside her on a silver ribbon of leash walks a trim Afgan hound with the same honey blond hair. Artemis throws back his head. A quiet high pitched moan rises from somewhere within as his left paw pounds uncontrollably against the railing. Hans is transfixed. The woman walks east down Sixth. The drunken masses seem to part like waves. She walks with her grand dog two blocks east, across the street and back up the south sidewalk, stopping only long enough to drop four crisp bills into the street drummer's kitty. Back at Congress Avenue, she crosses Sixth again and re-enters the Driskill, at which point Hans resumes breathing.

"She appears like clockwork at exactly eight minutes past the hour. That was the third time she did it. Intriguing isn't it?" Hans wonders aloud. His companion is leaning against the railing, his head resting on his paws, eyes closed, lost in a dream.

"I must know!" Hans shouts, startling Artemis back to reality. "No, I've outgrown lust. It's more curiosity. If I don't at least try to find the answer it may drive me to drink!"

Artemis snorts, shaking his head, and regains his footing on the rooftop. He knows it is a short drive. Having almost an hour to kill, Hans calls the waitress. "I'll have one more cognac and a bowl of water for my buddy then you can close out my tab. We're going to take a walk for awhile."

"I'll get your drinks and your check." She reaches down and gives Artemis a pat on the head. "I'll be right back."

Hans realizes that he will lose his observation post but is determined to solve this mystery. As Hans sips his final drink he thinks back to his long, happy marriage and how the years have slowed and thickened his once athletic body. "It's been a good run," he says, "and it ain't over yet!" He slaps the table with a new energy.

After paying his tab, Hans attaches the required but unnecessary leash to the leather harness surrounding Artemis. They enter the elevator. The musty cube is decorated with the dark walnut, burgundy velour and brass trim popular in the days of yore. It even has piped in elevator music, a sterilized version of a melody he and his young wife sang together years before while driving through the hill country. He can't quite remember the words. The ride ends too soon at street level where he will face the raucous throngs of drunken revelers. He looks at his watch. "We have a few minutes. Let's check out the scene." Hans adjusts his stature, infused with the energy of a new quest.

The evening is warm for a February, not uncommon for central Texas. The air is heavy with the smell of spilled beer and sweat. Otherwise intelligent college men are ejaculating strings of colored beads toward any glassy-eyed maiden who will reveal her mammary glands. Fueled by alcohol, hormones and drumming, the party is reminiscent of some medieval Pagan fertility festival. It's infectious if you are young. For men like Hans it's both silly and sad. For dogs like Artemis it's downright confusing. As they pass Sixth and Neches a tall cowboy is hurling verbal insults at a thick Middle Eastern male. The cowboy's drunken girlfriend hangs on him like a loose sweater. As the Middle Eastern man turns away she lacks the coordination to effectively flip him off.

"These are our leaders of tomorrow," Hans states.

He checks his watch, adjusts his tie and cufflinks, polishing them against the breast of his Brooks Brothers suit. "It's time to head over to the Driskill," he informs Artemis. He feels the blood in his ears and his pulse begins to race as the minutes tick away. His timing is impeccable. He reaches the corner of Sixth and Congress at exactly 7:08, just as the woman steps from the entrance.

"What a beautiful Afgan!" Hans recites his practiced line.

"Thank you. Her name is Sasha." The woman glances down at Artemis. "He's, um, quite a specimen also." She hesitates at "beautiful" which would be grossly inaccurate.

"This is my best buddy, Artemis. We have been partners for six years. Unfortunately, the old adage is true. I'm afraid we have grown to resemble each other as pets and their owners are prone to do."

The tall woman beams a genuine smile. "Well you both look very regal."

"I'm Hans, Hans Schickel."

"Lorraine Stewart." She extends her graceful hand which Hans takes gently in his.

"Very pleased to meet you. Would you walk with me?" They head east into the crowd. As they walk quietly for more than a block, Hans notices that Lorraine is not the young woman she appeared to be from a distance. The years have lighted on her like a butterfly, however, and a life of ease and privilege is obvious in her soft features.

"So what brings you to this decadent bacchanalia?" Hans eventually asks.

"I promised to meet someone," Lorraine replied. A brief cloud wafted across her countenance. Hans decides to just enjoy the walk.

As they approach the drummers, a girl of not more than 14 is slapping a tambourine. Two dark-skinned women in long gauzy skirts and tube tops are dancing teasingly around a tanned young man with long golden locks. He dances in a tantric trance, oblivious to his surroundings. A small crowd has gathered on the corner, fixated, their pulses attuned to the beat. Lorraine hands Sasha's leash to Hans. Pulling a five dollar bill from her small pocketbook, she steps through the throbbing crowd and deposits it in the tip jar. "That's for a friend who couldn't be here," she explains, noticing Hans' questioning stare. Hans is even more intrigued. Lorraine takes Sasha's leash and starts across the street, the same pattern as before.

Hans can't take it anymore. "I have to ask you something. I hope you don't think I'm out of line." Lorraine raises an eyebrow. "I was observing you from the top of that building earlier and I noticed that exactly the same time every hour, all afternoon, you walk this same loop."

"Really?" She looks surprised. "I didn't realize. I'm just trying to get Sasha used to the crowd. I have a room at the Driskill above the street and I want to leave my balcony door open tonight. I don't want her to be bothered by the noise. I find it stimulating."

"But exactly eight past the hour?"

"Seriously, it's coincidence. I'm surprised you noticed." She switches Sasha's leash to the hand nearest Han's and moves a slight distance away.

"Well, to be honest, you don't exactly fit in with this crowd. Not that that's a bad thing."

"Nor do you, sir. I don't see a lot of cuff links and Rolexes down here."

"I meant no offense. I tend to be more of an observer at these types of events. I'm afraid my days of lunacy are long passed," Hans says.

"I know what you mean, though I can't ever remember a time when I would have disrobed for a string of plastic beads." She exhales a gentle laugh.

Both humans simultaneously notice their canine companions making introductions in the dog appropriate head to tail position. "They seem to be getting on well," Lorraine mentions.

"Easy Arty!" Hans exclaims as Artemis places a meaty paw in the middle of Sasha's haunches.

"Oh, let them play. I'm surprised it took this long. Sasha is a bit of a flirt!" Lorraine is sizing up Hans, ignoring the frisky dogs. They pull the dogs apart and continue the short walk. Just before the final leg of the pre-ordained route Lorraine turns to Hans. "Would you like to come up? As I said, I have a balcony overlooking Sixth. It's only two floors up, an excellent observation point."

Hans extends his hands as if they are the scales of justice. "Well let's see, I could go home and rattle around my empty house or spend the evening with an intriguing woman. It seems obvious."

"Okay, then," Lorraine blushes ever so slightly at his boldness. She leads the way through the Romanesque entrance.

Once inside the room they unleash their companions who immediately lounge, noses almost touching, on the cool tile floor near the bathroom.

"Would you like a drink?" Lorraine asks.

"What do you have?"

"I have some very good tequila and, well ---I guess tequila is about it but I would be happy to call down for something else."

"Tequila is fine, although I'm not well versed on the customs surrounding it."

"Leave it to me," Lorraine states and removes two tiny shot glasses and a crystal salt shaker from her luggage. She steps over to the counter and dices a lime into eighths. She places it all on a tray and carries it to the balcony. "Tequila lessons," she says. She pours two shots, licks, then salts the back of her left hand, swallows the drink, flinging her head back dramatically, lashes the salt from her hand with a quick tongue and bites firmly into the lime, her eyes glowing. She indicates the remaining shot. "Your turn!"

Hans does his best to emulate her action. He decides that tequila was probably the worst tasting liquor he has ever experienced but the primal heat explains the glow in Lorraine's eyes.

They observe the street below. The drumming has intensified. The pulsating crowd is an organic rainbow of sparkling color. Primitive noises, punctuated by screams and grunts, echo down the concrete chasm as a spell is being cast over the city.

As Lorraine is refilling the shot glasses, Hans notes a pale circle around her ring finger.

"Are you married?" He blurts.

"Widowed, just last month."

"Oh, I'm sorry. That's terrible!" Hans tastes foot.

"Sad, yes, it was very unexpected, but ironic, really."

"What happened?" Hans asks, sensing she wants to talk about it.

"Arnold, that was my husband's name, was terrified of flying. He was an engineer so he realized it wasn't a rational fear. Still, anytime he had to board a plane he was certain it would be his demise. He would always tell me how much he loved me and what he would like me to do if he died. It became almost a morbid joke for us. January fourth, as I drove him to Love field to catch a charter flight, he started with the death thing again. I wasn't in the mood and I told him so." Lorraine drinks her shot sans salt and lime. She pours another shot. "The plane went down in the Ozarks. There were no survivors, at least not by the time help arrived. Anyway, that's why I'm here. We came down every year for Fat Tuesday and we already had reservations. One of the things he made me promise was to come here without him should he not return." She pauses for a moment and surveys the scene below. Setting free a reserved chuckle she picks up her glass and throws back the shot, forcefully. "So what about you?"

"I lost my wife six years ago. She had a long fight with breast cancer. Her name was Vena. She was a tiny woman with sparkling green eyes, curly red hair and more energy than any six toddlers you can imagine. She always seemed happy. I remember when she first found the lump. We were about to make a buying run through the mid-west. She owned an antique shop over on South Congress. I still have it. We were going to be gone for about three weeks. It was right after Christmas. I tried to get her to see a doctor. She said, 'There ain't enough titties here for cancer to bother with.' When we returned she was busy with inventory and taxes. She didn't get around to seeing the doctor for a couple of months. By that time it was too late. She fought hard, radical mastectomies, chemo, alternative therapies, the works. She lost all her hair and quit eating. That's when we bought Artemis. She had always wanted an English Bulldog but I had put her off. She had always wanted children, too, but I kept saying 'eventually'. At least she got the bulldog. She lasted about seven more months, four of them on Hospice. She might

~ 16 ~

have lasted longer but I couldn't stand to see her in so much pain. I encouraged the Hospice nurse to give her maximum doses of her pain meds. One day, after the nurse left, we finished off a bottle of her favorite wine and she just went to sleep. I sold my company to pay off the house and medical bills. I still run the shop she owned. I guess it's just a way to keep her memory fresh."

"I see you still wear your wedding ring," Lorraine observes.

"It won't come off. I was fairly lean when we were married. Age, I'm afraid, has thickened me. I guess I could have it cut off but I could never see the point."

They look out at the crowd again. Lorraine spots a young shirtless man, his body heavily inked in tribal tattoos. He dances wildly, his oily bronze curls slapping against his shoulders as he throws back his head. Dangling from his left arm are several dozen strands of colored beads. On his chest is stenciled a large crescent moon.

"Hey, moonchild," Lorraine yells down at him, waving the bottle in the air. "Would you like a shot of tequila?"

"Cool, Babe, I'll be right up!" The prancing boy replies.

"No need, just tilt your head back and keep your mouth and eyes open. I'm a pretty good shot with this thing but I may need some help from your end," she yells.

The young man plants his feet firmly on the ground and arches his back as if he is preparing to balance a billiard stick on his nose. "Give her a go!" Lorraine fills a shot glass and pours with flair. Except for the first tentative drops it is a direct hit.

"Awesome, darlin'," the boy hollers after swallowing the cactus juice. He takes a string of maroon beads from his wrist and slings it toward her like a lasso. She catches it on the bottleneck then slips it over her head. The boy dances away.

~ 17 ~

"Now everyone is going to think I've been running around half naked."

"Isn't it about time to walk the dog?" Hans asks, noticing it is approaching nine.

"They don't look like they want to go anywhere soon," Lorraine says, seeing both animals stretched out on the tile floor, sleeping peacefully.

"I wish I could sleep like that," Lorraine says. "Since Arnold died I just go through the motions. I don't even know why. I'm not sure there's a 'me' in here anymore, even if it matters."

"I'm not sure you ever lose that other part that comes with love," Hans says. "Myself, I've made a point to hold on. It was my best part but it is limiting. I guess we all handle it in our own way. If it makes you feel any better, it does get easier, -- slowly."

Lorraine studies Hans until he looks away from the street. When their eyes lock she doesn't turn away. "Why don't you guys stay the night?" She asks, pouring two more shots.

Hans again weighs his options, rattling around his Westlake villa or spending the night wrapped up with this fascinating woman. "I haven't been with a woman since Vena passed," he warns.

"Well it's about time don't you think?" Lorraine says.

"I guess it's like riding a bicycle."

"Let's hope not, but I guess if you can tell the handlebars from the pedals we'll be okay." Lorraine licked her hand and threw back the shot. Hans followed suit.

"Just curious, what made you pick out that boy for the tequila drop?"

"He reminded me of my son."

"You have a son?"

"Yeah, he's married. He lives in North Dallas. His wife is a physics professor at UNT. He's a professional photographer, pretty good at it, too. If you've read any national magazines, you've seen his work. You wouldn't think a scientist and a photographer would hit it off but I guess it's that they both have such a unique way of seeing things. He actually has an opening tonight at the 500 X Gallery. He's showing his photos from the Malaysian tsunami recovery efforts."

"Shouldn't you be there?" Hans asks, puzzled.

"I'll see them when I get home. He doesn't need his mother cramping his style at his big soirée." Lorraine takes Hans' meaty hand and holds it to her cheek. "Thanks for staying," she says and looks into his eyes. The drumming has reached a frantic pace. Lorraine places the half full bottle of tequila in the refrigerator leaving the patio door open.

Hans is nervous, but only until he's encircled in Lorraine's slender arms. He suddenly feels very much at home. Their lovemaking is passionate and energetic but comfortable. It's as if they have known each other since the beginning of time.

Hans falls asleep for the first time in years without longing for Vena's touch. Lorraine prays, not to God, but to Arnold. "I fulfilled my promises. Thank you for bringing me to this place. Amen."

*****

"Reggie, you need to get ready. The cab is scheduled for 830.

"Just a minute, Viv, I'm having trouble with one of my clocks again. It keeps gaining time." Reggie was fiddling with one of the dozens of antique clocks lining the walls of his studio.

"You can't gain time, at least not in this universe. It's just inaccurate," Vivian explains. She teased him with the subtle nuances.

"Spoken like a true physicist," Reginald replied, "but this little clock has gained eight minutes in the last two weeks. That's unacceptable."

"Can't you worry about it later? You have at least two devices on your person directly connected to the world atomic clock at the Naval Observatory." Vivian countered, though she knew her protestations were futile.

"It's strange, though. It gains eight minutes quickly then remains eight minutes fast, like it's on a different schedule. What could it mean?"

"Okay, which one is it?" Vivian chose to humor him for the sake of expediency.

"It's the one with the Romanesque façade that has the door that the woman walks her dog through on the hour."

"Isn't that the one we picked up in New Orleans?"

"No, we got it in Austin a few years ago when we met Mom and Dad for Fat Tuesday. Remember the little baldheaded woman with the shop on Congress?

"Oh yeah," Vivian remembered. "I wonder how she's doing. She was obviously sick with something. I remember she really wanted a good home for that clock. I thought it strange that she would have such an attachment to an object she was trying to sell."

"I can't figure it out. I guess I'll have to find someone to repair it. In the meantime it should take only a few minutes to recalibrate." Reginald continued to tinker with the clock.

"Can you hurry? You'll be late for your own opening!"

"Fashionably late."

"Maybe, but we did request a cab for 830."

"Please, Viv, just let me do this."

Vivian spun and left the room in a huff. Reginald reset the clock and dressed for his night out. He joined Vivian in the front hall. "Do you ever regret marrying a photographer?" He asked.

"I never regret marrying you," she said. Sometimes I don't understand what you do."

"You know more about how a camera works than I know about physics."

"Just because I know how a camera works doesn't make me a photographer. The camera has no more to do with photography than one of your clocks have to do with time. It's your eye and how it connects to your heart. That's what I love about you." They embrace.

"Opposites attract," Reggie smiled.

"See, you do know about physics." Vivian pressed her cheek to his chest. The cab arrived exactly on time.

*****

In less than a millisecond the rays emanate from the glowing pumpkin on the horizon. They pierce the atmosphere, ooze through the smog, dance off the bronze mirrored skyscrapers and slam to their death against the grey concrete three-story supporting Hans and his companion.

"It's almost time," Hans informs Artemis. The canine places his ample paws on the railing. Together they stare toward the entrance of the Driskill Hotel. Hans checks his Rolex. At exactly 6:00pm she emerges.

LIFE AMENDED

On July the third of 2008 Leticia Megan Boxholder
shimmied free of her mortal coil. It was ruled an accident but was
possibly exacerbated by the two hits of Ecstasy she had ingested and
the lack of blood in her alcohol stream. Apparently the disco lights
and the techno beat of the backup alarm drew her into another losing
relationship, this time with a garbage truck. The garbage truck made
out fine. Let Me, as she was known to her friends and associates, met
a quick and relatively painless demise. Her last words, had anyone
heard them, were "Damn, you stink!" She left behind a checking
account containing 279 dollars and odd change, a 1989 Mazda
pickup missing the driver's side window, a two bedroom Southside
apartment with rent that was three days in arrears and me, Shotgun
Willie Boxholder. I was well into my fourteenth year on this planet,
an only child and my mom's pride and joy. She claimed I was
fathered by Willie Nelson, the Red Headed Stranger of country
music stardom. I doubted it but I never told her that. For one thing, I
have blond hair, not red, and Mom's hair wasn't blonde unless you
count the few times she pulled an all-nighter with Miss Clairol. For
another, if Mr. Nelson had fathered all the children of all the
barmaids and waitresses that were attributed to him, he would never
have gotten into the studio long enough to produce even one single,
much less the hundreds of melancholy tracks he was famous for.
Still, my birth certificate reads Shotgun Willie Boxholder.

Let Me was what the hippies call a "free spirit" and what the rednecks called a "hippie". She loved everyone, spiritually, emotionally and physically as well. Her funeral was attended by somewhere near a thousand people. It was held outdoors on the shores of Lake Travis at Paleface Park sometime after the politically correct faction of the county government had renamed the park Pace Bend. The obituary said Paleface. Her ashes were scattered in the breeze not smoked as many suggested. I know, I was the one who let them fly. Any outsider who happened on the occasion might have thought someone had opened a wrecking yard on the site and, in fact, when the ceremony ended several sets of jumper cables were required to get folks on their way. A few hundred of her closest friends stayed on to "grieve" for a couple of days and try to figure out what to do with me. I've always found it strange how the poorest people are the most generous. When I left the gathering driving her old pickup, the bed was loaded with groceries, I had enough money to keep the landlord happy for a couple of months and almost an ounce of sticky Sinsemilla to get me through the "rough patch".

Regardless of what anybody said, my mom was awesome. Years of tending bar had given her a masters in philosophy from the school of hard knocks and yet she was the most positive person I had ever met. She had a couple of sayings that I was trying to hold on to in this time of confusion. One was "You have assets. We all do, Use 'em". Another one that had me a little apprehensive was "Change is inevitable, try to make it go your way". That one I was having trouble with. I was okay for now except for the losing my mom / best friend, but I knew the other shoe was bound to fall. I just didn't know when or where. I had been offered a couple of jobs by Mom's friends. One was landscaping which might be pretty cool. The other one was staying up all night cleaning high rise offices. The only positive thing about that was I could work on my Spanish. Anyone who had ever been in our house would assure you that my talents did not include housekeeping. I would have to take both jobs in order to keep the place we had and I had to sleep sometime not to mention school which I had no intention of quitting. Between school and life in general I knew enough about how the government worked to understand that the age thing was eventually going to bite me in the ass.

It must have been a week after mom's funeral, I was sitting on the couch, half way through getting over a "rough spot", when there was a knock. I emptied about a half can of aerosol pine forest into the atmosphere and opened the door. It was Zane. I had wasted the pine forest. Zane was one of Mom's more than friends. She really had a soft spot for him but she told me he was "too nice". She didn't want to see him get hurt so they kept it casual. He took a seat and I fired the joint back up. Zane had done a few years of pre-law at UT before his band had a meteoric one hit grand slam. They toured out of a van for about eight months then broke up to prevent an imminent homicide. Zane never made it back to school but he worked as a paralegal in one of the city's more aggressive law firms. Zane took a massive hit off the joint and held it longer than I thought anybody in a suit possibly could. He exhaled and turned his glassy eyes towards me.

"How would you like to be filthy rich?" He asked.

"I'm halfway there," I said. We both just lost it.

When we were able to catch our breath again he explained the situation.

"I've been talking with one of the attorneys at my firm and he thinks you could get a pretty good settlement from your mom's accident."

"Hell, even I know you can't sue the city without their permission," I said.

"True, but the truck that ran over your mom was an independent contractor, a big one, nationwide."

"No shit?"

"No shit. Plus, you've got to realize , you may be able to coast under the radar for awhile but you're 14. CPS will eventually be knocking at your door and no amount of air freshener is going to keep them from crawling up your ass."

"Yeah, I've thought of that. When Mom and I would get in too deep with the bill collectors we would just move. The post office rarely forwards mail addressed to Boxholder. I figure CPS is a little more persistent."

"Let Me would be devastated if she thought you would end up in state custody."

"So what's the plan?"

"You have family. What about your uncles?

"Mom has two brothers. Her older brother, Albert, is upstate in his second year of a ten year stretch for armed robbery. He could be out in 5 for good behavior but that's not his style. Her younger brother, Halsey, is a registered sex offender. He's actually pretty cool but I'm guessing the state wouldn't let me move in with him. It's sad, too, because it's kind of my fault."

"You can't blame yourself if he molested you."

"Oh, Hell no! He's 100% hetero. What happened was that I hooked my friend up with him. She was 13, almost 14 and he was 26. I covered for them with her parents, let them think I was her boyfriend. I don't really go for skinny chicks who sit in the dark and slice up their forearms with razorblades. They seemed to hit it off though. They were good for each other. She quit cutting and he got off of the crank. It was like love but when her dad found out he went looking for Halsey with a shot gun, turned him over to the police at gunpoint. Three days later they found the girl hanging in her closet. She's not dead but she might as well be. She just lays in bed and pisses on herself. They have to feed her with a tube."

"So you're on your own?"

"Pretty much. I figure I could make out fine by myself if not for the money thing. Mom let me handle a lot of the day to day stuff anyway. She sure as hell didn't want to mess with it."

"I'm thinkin' we can solve that problem. Stop by the office tomorrow morning. I want you to meet this attorney we have named Jack Montpier. He's a fucking piranha. I swear when I told him about your situation his eyes started glowing. He'll probably want a pretty hefty cut, thirty or forty percent, but sixty percent of something is better than a hundred percent of nothing."

"Sure, I'll stop by. It's not like I have a lot on my plate. You want to finish this before you split?"

"Why not? Are you holding up okay? Is there anything I can get for you?"

"I really miss her. Especially in the mornings. She used to get up and before she had breakfast or anything she would water all the plants and just sing to them, loud. I guess she was singing to me, too, although I never thought of it like that then."

"I miss her too. I always thought we almost had something a time or two."

"You know, she wanted to, but she liked you so much that she was afraid if it went south you might get hurt."

"It's a risk I would have gladly taken."

"I know." We didn't say anything else for fear our voices might crack, at least that's how it felt to me.

*****

The office was in a perfect historical restoration of a three story Victorian mansion on Rio Grande. The smell of leather and Old English lemon oil permeated the air. Though the temperature outside was already pushing the triple digits by 10:30, you could have hung a side of beef inside without fear of bacterial contamination. That was just the entry hall. As I closed the front door behind me, Receptionist Barbie looked up from her immaculately clean mahogany desk.

"You must be Mr. Boxholder, Mr. Montpier is expecting you. Right this way, sir."

I followed. She could have led me all over town and straight through the gates of Hell and I would have followed. They shouldn't let 14 year old boys loose with this many hormones. She went to the end of a hall and opened the last door. That ride ended too soon, I thought.

"Mr. Boxholder to see you, sir." And just like that she was gone. The opulence of this inner sanctum made the outer office look like a porta-potty.

"Good morning Mr. Boxholder. I'm Jack Montpier but just call me Jack. Have a seat."

"Call me Willie," I said and sat down. I was absorbed by a leather throne.

"I discussed your case with Zane. I hope you don't mind," Jack said. "I understand he is a close friend of the family?"

"We go way back."

"First let me say, I'm sorry for your loss and I deeply respect your decision to continue independently."

"I don't know how else to do it unless I end up living with strangers and that's not an option for me."

"That's one of the issues that is going to complicate this case. We can talk here as much as we want. We have attorney client privilege. Before we file any motions , however, you will be appointed a guardian ad litum. This is an adult, appointed by the court, with the responsibility to guard your interests. Invariably, because you are a minor, the Child Protective Service will get involved. The fact is, it's only a matter of time before they get involved anyway assuming you aren't going to drop out of sight. This is something we will need to deal with while the ball is still in your court."

"So what's the plan." I was thinking this might be a good time to run but the curiosity was getting the better of me.

"Do you have any family or close friends that could take you in or at least give the illusion of what we call conservatorship?"

"Sure, I have a lot of friends but not any that I can think of that would want the legal system all up in their business."

"That could be a problem."

"What about Zane?"

"I don't know. They usually want a couple."

"No, I mean for the added guardian whatever. I trust him."

"Maybe. We can check his credentials."

"My apartment is paid up two months in advance. Why can't I just stay there?"

"No adult supervision."

"Jack, I've been without adult supervision since I went off the tit."

"We're going to keep that between us."

"Isn't there a way I can be declared an adult?"

"Maybe if you were sixteen. Have you been in any trouble?"

"I'm incorrigible. It's in my permanent record since second grade."

"I mean legal trouble, misdemeanors, felonies."

"No, I've been lucky so far. I got stopped once driving Mom home from work but when the cop saw what kind of shape she was in he let me slide with a warning."

"I don't see any way we can proceed without putting you in a home, at least for a couple of years."

"Nobody is going to take a 14 year old who is incorrigible."

"In most cases I would agree but if you throw a million plus bucks into the equation the rules change."

"What the... How much?"

"I figure we can settle out of court for two million, maybe more. That would leave you with around one point two or better. My cut will only be 25% if we can keep it out of court."

"Holy shit, Dude! Why don't I just hire a butler!"

"Yeah, if only it were that simple. You have to have your ducks in a row before you get the money."

"Let's get Zane in on this. There has got to be a way we can work this out and I would feel better if he was in it from the start. He's the only friend I have with any legal sense."

"He's over at the courthouse. Let me get Marcy to take you to lunch. We can meet back here this afternoon." He hit the intercom. Marcy, darlin', can you take Willie to get some lunch? I need y'all back by one." In less than a minute Receptionist Barbie pranced through the door with a tooled leather handbag over her shoulder. "Take him somewhere nice," Jack said.

*****

Some days are better than others. Most of the recent ones had been pretty lame and a little scary. I felt a paradigm shift hovering in the air and I was trying to hold on to Mom's words of wisdom. Life had also taught me that, in general, if it seems too good to be true it's usually false. Just being here with Marcy on Jack's dime was surreal to the seventh power. If I had been even three years older I would have been barking up her tree. The fact was, I knew she was just doing her job. I decided to make it easier on her and keep the drooling to a minimum. Still it was hard to keep my eyes on the conversation. She told me she hoped that when she had a son he would grow up to be as responsible as I was. I came real close to just volunteering for the position. Even though that would have solved both of our problems, I didn't expect the courts would buy into the deal. She couldn't have been more than twenty-two. I was beginning to reflect on how happy Halsey had been in his little May - December thing when she mentioned her fiancé and showed me the humongous diamond that I had somehow managed to overlook. The prime rib was excellent. Marcy was outstanding company. She even let me hold the door for her as we left the restaurant.

*****

Back at the office Jack's door was open. He and Zane were discussing something that it appeared neither of them were having any fun talking about. He motioned me in.

"We have a situation," he said. That was a word I knew had always carried a negative connotation in my experience. "Leticia's estate is carrying over 25 thousand dollars in outstanding debt."

"What do you mean 'estate'?" I asked. When I thought of estate, I pictured a manicured lawn with a large rock mansion centered behind a reflecting pool. "All she ever owned was the old Mazda pickup."

"Estate, in this case, means what you leave when you die," Zane interjected. "Let Me left owing a shitload of money to folks. Sadly, the way it works is that now you owe it."

"Not exactly fair seeing how I'm too young to sign for any debt. From what Jack says I shouldn't have any problem paying it off though."

"It just complicates matters, more fingers in the pie," Jack said. "Zane is willing to be your guardian ad litum so that can work in your favor. I still can't see how you can live on your own. The judge will want you under state control at least until the debts are paid."

"Please! We have got to avoid that. You have no idea how incorrigible I can be," I said. I heard Zane snicker under his breath. I'm guessing he might have an inkling having virtually cohabitated with Mom and I over several short spells.

"Let's take a break," Zane said. He jumped up and left the room without waiting for a reply. Jack and I just shrugged at each other as we watched him through the window. He climbed in his little coupe and hauled it out of the parking lot. Jack spent the next few minutes unsuccessfully trying to reassure me that we could come up with a workable solution.

Probably only ten minutes had passed when Zane pulled slowly back into his assigned space. Both of the windows of the car were down and music was blaring out at full volume. I recognized it as one of the songs from his band's only CD, not the hit. It was a track about refusing to grow up that we had both particularly enjoyed. He ambled back into the office. I could tell by his eyes where he had been. I wondered if Jack knew, or cared. Zane picked the biggest, fattest leather chair on my side of Jack's desk and plopped his skinny butt in it. He pulled his left ankle up over his right knee and leaned back.

"I'm going to adopt this little shit," he stated. Time stopped.

"Well... okay, hmm." Jack muttered.

"That solves all the problems, right?" Zane asked.

"Yeah... Yeah, that pretty much does it. You okay with that, Willie?"

"Works for me," I said.

*****

So here we are, one tiny happy family. It's three years now and thanks to a self paced charter school I'm done with high school. I'll start UT in the fall, one semester before Zane finishes his law degree. Maybe we can ride to school together. We bought this cheap little two bedroom on the south side so we didn't have to deal with landlords. I still drive Mom's pickup although I had the window replaced. Other than school we decided to just sit on the one point six million we ended up with. It seems that having too much money makes people treat you differently so we don't tell anyone. We both work part time and only party on the weekends. Today is July 3rd of

2011. It's a melancholy anniversary for me, Zane ,too, I guess. There's about three dozen of us out here at the Let Me Memorial Barbeque and Beer Bust in Paleface park. I'm sitting on the tailgate of the Mazda looking out across the lake at all the swimmers and skiers and folks playing with their big ole dogs and all of a sudden I can feel Mom here, almost see her really. She's laughing and singing and flitting from one person to another like a hummingbird at a honeysuckle vine, her bare feet kicking up little puffs of dust in time with the music. I feel the truck shift slightly under me and look to find a young woman sitting beside me. She has the richest mocha colored skin and a crazy wild set of dreads. She takes a deep drag on a fatty and hands it to me.

"I never had a chance to meet your Mom," she says. "What was she like?"

COYOTE

The searing August sun cooked the spirits from the desert landscape. The turkey vultures languishing on the bare branches of the madrone trees nodded, patiently waiting. Occasionally one would take wing to cool itself in the updrafts from the valley floor where a creek bed of fractured dirt and bleached bones meandered.

Had Carlos tried to verbalize his cursing of God, no sound would have escaped past his swollen tongue. Indeed his vocal chords had long since dried to the texture of dead smilax vines. Damp sweat no longer soaked through his denim shirt, only a greasy sheen where the fat of his once ample body oozed through his pores. Chasing the shade in a deep *barranco,* Carlos escaped the brutal midday sun, preferring to move by night.

So this was the path of least resistance? Easy money? Carlos realized now that Miguel had conned him into compliance with the greedy scheme. The first two runs were uneventful. picking up two dozen *obreros* in *Cuidad Acuna,* letting them ride in the back of the refrigerated produce truck. They traversed the border at the tiny Amistad Dam crossing, manned by only two guards, one of which was Miguel's brother-in-law, virtually assuring an uneventful crossing. It was a chance to give a better life to men. The men would be safer and make enough money to send home to their families. In exchange for this altruism, Carlos received nine hundred dollars for ten hours work. They dropped their charges off at a Dallas safe house where the money guys paid the balance and gave them their next assignment.

This last run was different. When they arrived at the pickup point 40 miles south of *Acuna,* the cargo was female. Eighteen young women awaited them. Several appeared to be dressed for a night on the town. Carlos knew he should have abandoned the project at this point. His experiences with women had been less than positive. His few attempts to relate to girls in high school had left him stung and shamed. His mama's wisdom about respecting women had not served the plump little introvert well. These women they were to transport were flamboyant and teasing, several offering "favors" for the privilege of riding up front. Carlos understood that even hookers could make a better life in the U.S. but he suspected Miguel's fascination with the seedy side of culture was the real reason for his decision to carry the girls. Two of the women were out of place in the group. An older woman and a girl of about fourteen, who appeared to be her daughter, stood away from the group, their eyes averted. They were dressed in the embroidered cotton dresses common to the working class of northern Mexico. Their calloused fingers lacked the painted nails of the other women. The older woman was beyond the age normally considered by men wanting to purchase companionship. She also had a dark spirit that made her disturbing and unapproachable. Carlos was drawn to the distinctive Mayan features of the daughter, a girl with high cheekbones and full lips.

"Why women, Miguel? What are we to do with these women?" Carlos asked.

"Just a different kind of *las trabajadora.* Supply and demand, you know, land of opportunity and all that."

"Well I don't like it! Someone could take advantage of those two *campesinas*."

"It's not for us to say. The pay is good, no?"

"Sure but...."

"No buts, we take them. They've made the down payment."

"This is wrong!" Carlos said.

"No, this is life, same job, better environment, better pay, everybody wins."

"But what about the mother and child?"

"She doesn't look like a child to me. I wish she wanted to ride up front. I could work something out for her."

"You're a sick bastard."

"Why? You want her? I can make that happen."

"Let's just load up and go." Carlos had a brief image in his mind. He was on top of the naked girl but he saw only fear in her eyes. He shook his head violently to make the image fade. He helped the women into the truck, pulled down the overhead door, latched it and affixed a fictitious Department of Agriculture seal. Sliding his machete behind the seat, he climbed into the passenger side and they hit the road.

When they reached the border crossing Miguel pulled into the parking area and jumped out of the driver's seat.

"Ronaldo! My brother! *Mi hermana* treating you right? You don't look like you miss any meals." Miguel slapped the pudgy little man affectionately on his wide back.

"She's getting meaner every year but I can still out run her," Ronaldo said, giving Miguel a hug. "What are you hauling today?"

"I've got a truckload of hookers headed for New Orleans."

"Yeah, right. Seriously, *cunado*?"

"Lettuce, already inspected and sealed." Miguel waved a hand toward the truck.

"So, are you ever going to settle down, start a family?"

"Not likely. I don't need some damn woman running my life. I'm doing fine on my own."

"Who's riding with you?" Renaldo asked, pulling a notepad from his pocket.

"Carlos, Juanita's boy. He needed a summer job," Miguel replied. "He's only sixteen, but he has a license so we trade off at the wheel. More miles, more money, you know the story. Speaking of, I better head out."

Ronaldo put the notepad away. He went around and fingered the steel band threaded through the latch. "Don't let me hold you up. See you Thanksgiving if not sooner. Be careful!"

"You, too. Give Marissa my love."

Once back in the U.S., Miguel decided to stay to the back roads to avoid the checkpoints. One section of their route took them 40 miles through a hunting lease on a road that wasn't on a map. It saved 25 miles and avoided a checkpoint, a slow rough ride over a road that varied from a path to non-existent. By the tenth mile the women in the cargo box were yelling and beating on the walls. Miguel was trying to ignore them.

"Aren't you going to do something?" Carlos asked.

"Maybe you were right about hauling these women. They sure are a noisy bunch, They can make all the noise they want out here but I'll need to shut them up before we get back to civilization." Miguel said.

"I've never had anything but trouble with women," Carlos said. A minute later a loud thump was heard from the box followed by a blood curdling scream.

"Maybe this will shut them up." Miguel reached under the dash and flipped the cargo light switch, plunging the women into total darkness. After a couple of shrieks the voices became noticeably quieter. Soon a rhythmic thumping began and the truck began to rock back and forth.

"These God damned bitches are trying to flip the truck!" Miguel screamed. He stopped the truck, turned on the cargo light and reached into the glove box, pulling out a 9MM Berretta. "I've got to stop this shit!" He jumped out of the truck. "C'mon, bring your machete."

Carlos followed orders, popping the seal from the latch with the large knife. Miguel slung the overhead door open.

"What the hell is going on here?" Miguel screamed.

One of the women jumped out. "This old *bruja* conjures. See! Ants, all over me!"

"I don't see anything."

The mother of the young girl was laying, half-conscious, against the wall of the box, blood streaming from behind her ear. The frightened girl was kneeling over her.

"What happened to the *campesina*?" Carlos asked.

"She fell," the woman stated. The other women looked away.

"What's your name?" Miguel demanded.

"What do you care?"

"Give me your fucking name!" Miguel shouted and pointed the Berretta at her face.

"Rosa," she said.

"Take her around front of the truck. I'm going to see if I can help this woman."

Carlos motioned with the machete. Rosa slunk to the front of the truck. "I was just trying to give the *chica* some pointers, let her know what to expect. Her mama hexed me. I swear."

"Shut up! I didn't bring you up here for a conversation," Carlos said. He heard the door of the cargo box close.

Miguel came around the truck. "She's in pretty bad shape. The bleeding slowed. She might make it. This bitch beat the shit out of her, probably because she wanted to recruit the daughter."

"The witch has no clue to what's going on," Rosa said.

"Shut up! You're the problem!" Miguel barked. "Carlos, tie her up and put her in the truck."

"No," Rosa cried. "Don't put me back in there with her ... I can't..."

"Fine, Mexico is that way." Miguel pointed the gun south. "Del Rio is that way." He shifted the barrel slightly eastward. "Move it!"

"No, no, I'll die! Please let me ride up front with you. I won't be a problem."

"You're already a problem."

"I can make your journey very enjoyable."

"Yeah, so can anyone back there. You're not my type."

"But I'll die in the desert."

"Probably, but if you don't start walking I'm drop you with one shot and the buzzards can have you."

Rosa turned to leave then spun around and spit toward Miguel. The explosion from the Berretta echoed through the valley as Rosa dropped in a clump at Carlos' feet.

"God damn, Miguel! What the fuck! Are you ... you killed her!" Rage was causing Carlos to shake.

"Let's go." Miguel turned toward the truck. Carlos was unable to move. The machete fell from his hand, the handle dropping heavily against Rosa's lifeless cheek.

"I said, let's go," Miguel barked. Carlos bent down and picked up the machete. He lunged forward. Miguel raised the gun toward Carlos. "That's not a good plan," Miguel stated coldly. "We need to leave." Miguel closed the cargo door and climbed into the driver's seat. Carlos was still trembling when Miguel started the truck.

Soon they were bumping along the path. No one talked. Carlos was unable to reconcile the recent events with the cousin he had grown up with, playing soccer and eating barbequed *cabrito* on the weekend. Miguel had always organized the games and ruled them with his athletic prowess. When the other uncles and cousins were getting married and becoming tools of their women, Miguel drove a new pickup and restored a '72 Corvette, always had money and lived large. He had been Carlos' favorite cousin. Now the man at the wheel seemed like a stranger with the arid landscape sliding past his gaunt features. The road was no longer visible. Only a crooked line on a hand held GPS kept them headed through the desolation. The truck began shuddering with the slightest acceleration. An ominous clicking sound was coming from somewhere underneath. Miguel stopped to inspect the problem. When he crawled from under the truck the color had drained from his face.

"U-joint. It's about to give out." He consulted the GPS. If we turn around, it's eleven miles back to the highway and another 10 or so to the closest town or it's 25 miles to the highway ahead but there's a town with a garage at the junction. I say we go for it. It's six of one , half a dozen of the other."

"Will we make it?" Carlos asked.

Miguel just shrugged. "We could lighten our load. It might help, but we wouldn't get the rest of our money."

"No! We're in the middle of the desert."

"Then let's move out."

After a half hour of creeping down the path with the noise getting no worse, the two men relaxed. Miguel decided to pick up the pace. As soon as he reached 20 miles per hour the u-joint gave way with a loud pop and the truck rolled to a stop.

"Shit!" Miguel shook his head and stared through the windshield. Carlos watched him, looking for some sign of action. Miguel just stared ahead. Finally he checked his cell phone. He climbed on top of the cargo box. After spinning a couple of 360 degree pirouettes with the phone held high, he flipped it closed with a resigned sigh. "No service."

"What are we going to do?" Carlos asked. Miguel pulled the pistol from the glove box.

"No!" Carlos screamed.

"What? I'm not going to shoot anyone but they aren't going to want to hear what I have to tell them. I may need backup. Bring your machete."

Miguel rolled open the door to the cargo box. The women, upon seeing the pistol, huddled near the front of the box.

"Nobody is going to hurt you but I need you to get out of the truck," Miguel insisted. The wary women kept their eyes on the men as they climbed down from the cargo box. Miguel stood aside holding the pistol while Carlos helped each woman negotiate the long step down. Only the injured woman and her daughter remained. The older woman appeared barely conscious and the girl glared defiantly, refusing to exit the vehicle. Carlos had one foot on the step when Miguel stopped him. "Let them be for now. Close the door." Carlos followed orders.

"Ladies, the truck is dead," Miguel said." It's going to take some time to get it fixed. We don't have enough food and water to keep you. If you follow the path back the way we came it's just over 10 miles to the paved highway. None of you pretty ladies should have any trouble getting a ride."

"What about our money? You were supposed to take us to New Orleans," one of the women asked.

"We got you across the border. That's the best we can do. You're on your own now. It's about a 4 hour walk. If you keep a good pace you should make it to the road well before dark. I suggest you girls get moving."

The women stood for a moment and consulted in hushed tones. Miguel cocked back the hammer on his pistol and the conversation died.

"Give us some water?" asked the woman who had spoken earlier. Carlos took a jug from the cab of the truck and handed it to her. She turned to Miguel.

"P*endejo!* You are the worst *coyote* in Texas, maybe the world! You should be ashamed taking advantage of us."

Miguel looked genuinely offended. "Look, it's the best we can do under the circumstances. I'm sure most of you will be fine. Consider it an adventure."

The women left in a group following the tire tracks back toward the horizon. The men watched them leave.

"What about the other two?" Carlos asked.

"I guess we'll keep them until help arrives."

"No one knows where we are except the women and I doubt they will say"

"We have a phone and a GPS, enough water for a couple of days and fuel to run the refrigeration system."

"Right. But we have no service and what about the *campesinas?*"

Miguel leaned against the truck and pinched the bridge of his nose. Carlos waited. Miguel was silent. Carlos needed a minute to think. He opened the cargo door.

"What are you doing?" Miguel asked.

"I'm going to check on the old woman." Carlos motioned the daughter out of the box, leaned the machete in the corner and kneeled down by the prostrate woman. He held his fingers to her throat. Her heart was beating very rapidly. "What's your name?" He asked. She just stared. He repeated the question in Spanish. No answer. He felt her forehead. It was cool but clammy. He saw her lips move. He drew his ear close to her mouth. The words she uttered were clear but in a language that was unfamiliar. When he looked at her again, her eyes appeared to glow. They burned through him. A physical pain ignited in his arms and legs. He had to get away! He jumped down from the box just as Miguel grabbed the girl by the back of the head and pulled her to him.

"Miguel! Stop!" Carlos shouted.

"Hey, Cuz, we're going to be here for a while. We might as well have some fun."

"The old woman is dying! We need to get help. leave her alone."

Miguel released the girl and turned on Carlos. "I'm running this operation! You will not tell me what to do!"

"That doesn't seem to be working out too well," Carlos countered. Miguel took a step toward him and slammed the Berretta hard against Carlos' ear. Carlos saw an image of the old woman shimmer and fade as his knees buckled. When he regained consciousness Miguel was leaning over him with a damp rag pressed to his temple.

"Damn, Cuz, I guess you forgot I had the gun in my hand. Are you okay?"

Carlos wanted to strangle Miguel but his arms felt like limp sausages and his head throbbed.

"Fuck you," he whispered.

Miguel grinned. "You're okay." When Carlos staggered to his feet he noticed the girl was tending to her mother and Miguel was studying the GPS, writing some numbers on a card from his wallet.

"See that rise?" Miguel pointed to an outcropping of rock about a mile away "I want you to take the phone and climb up there. Hopefully you can get a signal. Call this guy. His name is Julio. He lives in Beeville. We can trust him. Give him our coordinates from here on the back of this card. Tell him our situation. He'll pick us up."

"The women?"

"Fuck 'em, not my problem at this point."

"Why me? You go!"

"You need the exercise, fat boy. Now move!" Miguel waved the gun.

Carlos knew why he was selected to go but he didn't want to be a pile of dry bones. He took the phone and a canteen of water and began his trek toward the mountain. He was less than a quarter mile away when the muffled screams reached his ears. He tried to focus on the mountaintop through the tears and picked up his pace.

The mountain seemed to move away as he approached. It must have been an hour before he reached the foot of the incline. At least the screaming had stopped. The climb was rugged but Carlos knew his life was in the balance. As he ascended, he checked for a signal every few hundred yards. Nothing. The terrain was barren but beginning to level out when he finally got a signal. He pulled out the card and dialed. A woman's voice answered.

"Hello?"

"May I speak with Julio please?"

"Just a minute." A minute passed, then two.

"Hello?"

"Julio?"

"Yes." The phone beeped. The battery indicator was flashing.

"I'm Carlos, Miguel's cousin. We're broke down in the desert. We need help. I have coordinates."

"Let me get a pencil"

"Hurry, my battery is going dead!"

There was no further communication. When Carlos looked at the screen it was blank. He pressed the power button. The face of the old woman materialized on the black screen. His arms and legs felt the shooting pain again.

"Holy Christ! God Damn!" he screamed and threw the phone. He collapsed in the dust, balling up from the pain.

When he could move his limbs again, he began the torturous climb down. He didn't want to go back to the truck but there was nowhere else to go. At least, if Miguel shot him, it would be a quick death. The canteen was dry and his legs were burning as he approached the truck. He saw the girl standing by the back of the truck with a blanket laid across the tailgate. Her dress had been ripped down the front. She had cut strings from the fabric to tie it closed.

"Is help coming?" she asked.

"No. Where's Miguel?"

She pointed into the cargo box. His cousin was lying face down in a puddle of blood, the machete buried in his rib cage.

"My God! What have you done?"

"My mother saved me. He raped me. He was going to kill me. It took her last breath but she saved me. Now I will take her home."

Carlos just stared at his cousin's body. The girl climbed into the truck and lifted her mother's body, placing it gently on the blanket. Carlos saw the woman's eyes staring into nothingness. He reached for her face to close them. The girl grabbed him by the wrist. "No!" she said." She still sees. She's going to be my guide."

"She's dead. She can't help you. We can figure something out together."

"You don't know *mi madre*. She's with me. We're going home."

"You'll die in the desert."

"No, I'm from the desert. It's you who will die in the desert."

Carlos had heard stories of the native people of Mexico traveling hundreds of miles through barren terrain, but this child, carrying a body? "Please, leave her. Come with me. We can survive together."

"I owe her my life. We are going home."

"Wait!" Carlos filled his small canteen from the remaining gallon of water and handed it to the girl.

"Bless you," she said and turned to follow the tire tracks south, her mother's body draped over her shoulders.

Carlos left the refrigeration unit on. He covered Miguel's body with a blanket and sat in the corner of the cargo box to figure out his strategy. As the refrigerated air fell on him he realized how tired he was. He would rest. Then decide.

When he awoke, dusk had worked magic on the desert. He stepped from the box into the cool of the evening. The brightest stars were piercing the purple sky. The unseen life was producing whispers of sound in the still, dry air. Carlos gathered the GPS, the last blanket and the rest of the water. He took almost eleven hundred dollars from Miguel's wallet leaving a single silver dollar he found behind the driver's license. Taking that would be stealing, he thought. It took him a few minutes to comprehend the technology of the GPS but after locating the map with the trail on it he proceeded. Twenty six point eight miles to civilization, he should be there by sunup. There was barely a sliver of a moon but his eyes adjusted to the starlight as the amber glow receded over the horizon. He had learned his lesson from the phone. He checked the GPS and took his bearings. The moon over his right shoulder would keep him on track. He turned off the GPS. As the screen faded the old *campesina's* haunted face appeared and the burning pain shot through his extremities bringing him to his hands and knees in the dust. Slowly the pain left his body and he was able to stand. Moon to the right, he trudged on.

The still desert air grew cooler. Carlos draped the blanket around his shoulders. The moon rose higher in the sky. Soon he would have to check his bearings.

He turned on the GPS and brought up the map screen. There was no trail. He enlarged the coverage and found the trail off to his left about three quarters of a mile. He picked up his pace and left the unit on until he rejoined the trail. By the dim light he could make out what might be a set of wagon tracks snaking off into the distance. He decided to follow it. It seemed to be the road. Again he turned off the GPS. This time he turned the screen away from him. Where the light from the screen shone, the sand formed a crystalline face and pain shot up through the soles of his shoes, knocking him off his feet. He lost consciousness. When he awoke he noticed the water jug on its side. Most of the water had spilled out. The horizon was glowing to the east. Terrified, he gathered his things and began jogging down the wagon trail. Soon the trail became so faint he wasn't sure it was a trail or just lines of erosion in the sand. A deep *barranco* lay ahead that he knew no wagon or truck could cross. He would have to turn the GPS on again. Again no trail. He expanded the map. Still no trail. He expanded again. At the edge of the screen was the trail, over two miles to his right. This wasn't working. He would leave the unit on and try to intersect the trail ahead. He turned slightly to the right and set a course. His legs were aching. The sun was still touching the horizon but he was already sweating. He trudged ahead.

The sun was well into its searing arc when the GPS said he had intersected the trail. He couldn't see any sign of vehicular traffic and the trail began a sharp incline. He had the uncomfortable feeling that someone was watching him, toying with him like a rat in a maze, but there was no sign of life in any direction. He began his ascent, paying close attention to the screen. He had no intention of turning it off. He enlarged the coverage until he saw where the trail intersected the main road. He still had thirteen miles to go. His heart sank. He forged ahead.

The climb was steep. Sweat dripped from his nose and sizzled in the sand. The battery indicator on the GPS said he was at one quarter. As he crested the rise he located a rock formation straight ahead to fix on. He got down on his knees and elbows facing the formation. He placed the screen of the GPS against the sand and pressed the power button. The pain was blistering. He vomited. He heard the old crone inside his head speaking the odd language just before he fainted. When he woke up sand and vomit were dried on his face. His neck and ears were stinging from ants. He cursed Miguel. He cursed God. He cursed the old woman that haunted him, whose strange language still gurgled in his brain. He sipped at the few ounces of water in his jug. It burned his swollen tongue. He tried to locate the rock formation he had fixed on. That one, maybe, or the one just to the left. He couldn't be sure. He set out for the formation on the right.

Time passed and the formation didn't seem to be getting any closer. His legs were shaking and he was soaked in sweat. There was a *barranco* a hundred yards to the left. He needed rest, and shade. He stumbled to the dry wash, curling in the shadows and sipping some water. He dozed lightly, repositioning out of the sun, until dusk was near. Before dark settled in he crawled from his encampment like the other animals of the desert. He followed his footprints back to the trail.

He looked toward the rock formation that had been his reference. He wasn't sure. The voices were silent. "Please, God, a sign," he prayed. A falling star dropped from the heavens straight toward one of the formations. That could not have been a coincidence. He was certain. He fixed his eyes on the mark and trudged across the vast desert plain. The night grew darker and cooler. He wrapped in the blanket and drank the last of the water. Surely he would reach the road by morning. The sky was growing lighter as the huge formation loomed before him. He must be close. Carlos activated the GPS. The battery meter began flashing as he pulled up the map screen. The trail was about a half mile to the left but no intersection. He expanded the map screen, twice. The intersection came into view just as the screen flashed "Low battery - Shutting down". It looked like about 3 miles, a little curve to the left. The tingling began in his hand and came up his arm. He dropped the dead GPS. It was too late. Pain racked his body but he maintained consciousness. The burning did not want to leave. The old crone's voice was screaming in his head, repeating the same phrase in the strange language. Carlos squeezed his hands to his ears and thrashed his head about trying to silence the demon woman. The pain was searing, cooking his bones to dust. Slowly he returned to normal. He was crying like a child.

That was the last he heard from the old woman, or God, or man. That was yesterday. He tried to use the sun as a compass but he never found the trail again, or the road. He could barely move. He wandered by night, generally north, he hoped.

The sun is up. The turkey vultures advance. He tries to raise his arm to shoo them away but only his fingers move. A vulture lunges and rips one free. The pain barely registers. Another hops onto his chest. It stares into his eyes, cocking its head to one side. Those eyes, those same eyes as the old woman. He tries to laugh but his last breath is only a sigh as the vulture's beak steals his vision.

PAINTING OVER STAINS

I.

I'm stumbling and worn from a controlled blood loss. It pays thirty dollars and a glass of orange juice, enough money for hamburger, buns, tomatoes and bananas to last a few days. I'll have to choose between a bottle of cheap wine and fuel for the camp stove. I'm not quite out of fuel. I trade my room in the motor lodge for painting and drywall, general maintenance. It seems that no jobs exist for an ex-navy E-3 who was honorably discharged after a year. I couldn't handle endless hours on the ocean living in quarters the size of a coffin. Now I wonder if maybe I should have tried harder to hang in there, but my mind was slipping, like now.

I've done about all I can with the motel. It's pristine, for what it is. My conscience won't let me work any slower. Down the road the bridge is out and the river is flooded. The bottle of wine smoothes out the ripples in my brain but empties my pockets. My old Chevy sits outside my room gathering dust; tags expired, inspection out in two more months. It would run if it had gas. I could sell it for a few hundred if I could find the title. I may need to sleep in it soon.

II.

The painting is finished. The grounds are spotless. "We need the room back," he says. He's sorry, he says. I hand him the key. "Good luck," he says and looks away. "I'll pick up the car later," I say. "Cool," he says. I walk toward the blood center again. The water has receded. Men in hard hats and orange vests are cleaning up the debris. I begin to pitch in for something to do. A fat man leaning on a shovel motions toward me so I walk over.

"Where's your hard hat?" he asks.

"I don't have one," I say.

""You're supposed to have one."

I look up. There's nothing overhead. "I'm just helping for something to do," I say.

He looks at me as if I were some alien life form. "OSHA regs," he says.

"I'll get one if you give me a job."

"We only hire temps."

"I can be a temp."

"We go through an agency. They do drug tests and background checks."

I look around at his crew then look back at him as if he were space junk. "Which agency?" I ask.

"Hargrove," he says.

"I'm on their list," I say, "but they never tested me or called me about a job."

"What's your name?" he asks.

"Paul Thorndale" I say.

"If someone quits I'll ask for you," he says.

"Aren't you going to write my name down?"

"I'll remember," he says. I go back to picking up debris. "You have to leave," he says.

III.

The nights are getting chilly. I'm thankful that my Chevy is so old it has a front bench seat. My clothes, stove and few other belongings fill the back. After buying a quarter tank of gas, I have enough blood money left to do laundry so I clean up and shave in the bathroom of the washateria. I look okay, a little loose around the edges. Tomorrow I'll try to find work again.

IV.

I'm in the parking lot of the Home Depot when the sun comes up. A guy with a bent nose and jowls pulls up in a crew cab pickup. He's looking for painters, eight dollars an hour. He hires me. I climb in the cab. It smells like stale cigars and sour beer. "You speak Spanish? he asks.

"Muy poquito," I joke. He pulls around behind the store where three Hispanic guys wait. Two are young but one is old enough to be my grandfather. They jump in the bed of the truck before it comes to a complete stop, the two young guys grabbing gramps by both arms.

"What's your name?" bent nose asks.

"Paul," I respond. He asks me about my experience. "Just got out of the Navy," I say. "We painted anything that we didn't have to kill first." It was a joke but apparently bent nose didn't get it. Sometimes lately I feel like a refugee from an alien invasion. He tells me his name is Buddy. I doubt it but it makes no difference as long as he pays cash. We drive across town to an old neighborhood that seems to be experiencing gentrification where we stop at a single story frame house. Buddy pulls a metal sign from the back seat and plants it in the yard. It says Buddy's Painting and Drywall and has a phone number. He hands out paint scrapers and paper particle masks. "Wear them, the exterior tested positive for lead," he says, like it was an infection. He unloads a 5 gallon water jug and leaves. We get to work. The sun is low in the sky when he shows up to retrieve us. My elbows, shoulders and back feel demolished. I have blisters on my fingers and palms that have long since burst. He gives me three twenties and a ten. He gives Gramps a roll of bills. I had already determined that my three *compadres* were a familial unit. He gives us all a ride back to the Home Depot.

My car is gone. I go straight to the customer service counter. I have to throw a fit and a few items from the general area before I find someone who knows what's going on. "We had it towed," he states, "company policy. The tags were out, probably wouldn't have noticed if you hadn't parked at the edge of the lot."

"I was trying to leave the closer spaces for your customers," I say.

"Sorry," he says and hands me a card for the towing company.

"Can I use your courtesy phone?"

"Customers only," he says. I consider homicide but decide to walk away. Although the store is full of potential weapons, he is much larger than me and who knows what he has stashed behind that counter.

V.

Across the interstate from Homer's I find a convenience store with a working pay phone. The ten dollar bill is transformed into a bottle of cheap wine and a handful of quarters. " How much to bail out the old Impala?" I ask the wrecker guy, trying to maintain a jovial demeanor.

A gruff voice replies, " Ninety bucks, if you pick it up by midnight."

"I can't be there 'til tomorrow," I say.

"One hundred twenty, tomorrow," he says and hangs up. I find the address of the towing company on a map stuck to the wall inside the store. It's not quite five miles away. I can walk that, I'm thinking.

"You can't have that wine open in here," the kid behind the counter says. I hold the bottle straight out with my left hand and screw the lid on with my right. "You know what I mean," the kid says. "Get the fuck out before I call the law." I start toward him. He cowers against the back wall. I lean on the counter, my body bent at the waist. "Kiss my ass!" I turn and walk out the door, waving goodbye with one expressive middle finger.

VI.

The juniper tree behind the Home Depot blocks the final rays of the sun while the grape loosens the tight coils and spurs creative

~ 57 ~

contemplation. There's an abundance of cardboard available. I enter Homer's and spend a few of the quarters on a fat permanent marker. My sign says: "GET THIS HOMELESS BUM OUT OF TOWN! I need 50 more bucks to get my car out of hock!" Okay, maybe I lie a little. I'm not going anywhere soon but the sign works. Three hours on the street corner and I have another 60 bucks and I have yet to be seen by anyone I know. I start walking.

VII.

I never would have thought I would be so happy to be driving the old Chevy. I still have a few bucks in my pocket. Back at Home Depot I find a spot right in the middle of the parking lot, windshield facing east. Crack of dawn and I'm up looking for Buddy. About 8:30 he shows up, hung over as hell. I had received a couple of offers for painting gigs but I wanted to talk to Buddy. Most of the guys supposedly still looking for work really aren't. They either want too much money or they're obviously junkies. "How about this?" I ask Buddy. "You give me ten bucks an hour. I'll follow you to the jobsite and you won't have to bring me back. Come by and pay us at the end of the day and I'll bring the other guys back too." He looks at me sideways then looks around at the deadbeats gathered around his truck. "I'll make sure the job gets done," I say. I didn't know if I could pull it off but figured I had nothing to lose.

VIII.

It's three days later and I'm some kind of foreman I guess. I'm getting my ten an hour and I'm running the spray rig. It's me and the same three guys almost every day. If we need an extra I let Gramps pick somebody he knows. It's worked well so far. Buddy sits in his truck drinking beer and listening to sports on his satellite radio. Sometimes he splits for a few hours. Once in a while he gets out and stumbles around the jobsite pointing out this or that faux pas. We're starting another house tomorrow. It will be Friday. When we finish cleaning up the jobsite, Buddy collects from the homeowner. He gives me a hundred dollar bonus when he pays the day labor. I have 400 dollars in cash. I've been hanging on to it, sleeping in the car. Tonight I'm going back to the motel and see if I can work a weekly rate on a room.

IX.

Friday morning I'm at Homer's, showered, shaved and wearing clean clothes. I round up my regular guys and we share a box of donuts I picked up. It's 9 a.m. and still no sign of Buddy. The two younger guys take other work. I'm down to Gramps and some underage kid that's been hanging close. Buddy rolls up at about 9:45. He hands me a card with an address on it and gives me directions, says he'll meet us later. He smells worse than I did yesterday. There's a woman in the truck with him who's young enough to be his daughter. I'm pretty sure she's not. She looks rougher than he does.

We get to the house and unload our tools. "Where's Buddy?" the homeowner asks.

"He'll be by later," I say. "He had some business to take care of."

"He was supposed to be here."

"I don't know what to tell you. We're here, ready to go." The homeowner paces a couple of times around the yard, looking between me and the house. I wait.

"Okay," he says, "let me know as soon as he gets here."

We get to work. The homeowner comes out periodically to observe. It's almost 3 p.m. before Buddy shows up. He's had a shower but he's still wearing the same clothes. At least he's alone. The homeowner is out the door before the truck stops. We keep working but I'm trying to hear what's going on. It ain't pretty, but the energy winds down and they reach some agreement. Buddy calls us over. "Let's knock off for today, meet here Monday with the whole crew." He gives us each 50 bucks. "It's all I've got on me," he says. "I'll hook y'all up on Monday. Cool?" What could we say? I give the guys a ride back to Homer's, trying to appease them as we go. Truthfully, I'm concerned. I pick up a six pack and go chill at the motel. I plan on spending most of the weekend in bed.

X.

There's 100 channels on the cable TV and nothing worth watching. I swear this mattress was more comfortable a couple of days ago. It's Saturday afternoon and I'm antsy, not a good sign. When I get like this I usually get stupid. I decide to hedge my bets. I pay for an extra week at the motel, fill up the Chevy and stop by the A&P. I buy some fruit and three microwave entrees, all that will fit in the freezer of the minifridge.. A jumbo pack of jerky, some peanut butter cheese crackers and a twelve pack of PBR finish off the tab. By the time I get back to my room I've got less than 50 bucks left. Seriously, how much trouble can I get in for 40 dollars?

XI.

Fishing. That would be a good way to spend a Sunday. I don't have a pole or tackle. I figure when I get my own apartment and a thousand bucks in the bank I'll call my parents and let them know I'm okay, because, then, I really will be. My dad used to take me fishing, largemouth bass. He had the cool boat, fish finder, all the bells and whistles. I never really understood the fascination. Now I miss that. I'd give my left nut to be out on the lake with him right now, stalking the stripers.

Just to get out of the room I decide to take a stroll down by the river. I see people jogging on the path, older folks, with their grandkids, feeding stale bread to the ducks. There are a few homeless guys, nobody I know, sitting under the bridge passing the bottle. No one is fishing. Finally, I see a guy about my age showing his son how to catch perch. They have a couple of cane poles and some red wigglers. Whenever they catch one they throw it back.

XII.

I made it through the weekend unscathed. I'm here at Homer's at the butt crack of dawn, donuts in hand. After Friday it's going to be tough to round up my crew. They show, so before they have a chance to ask questions, I pile them in the Chevy and head for the jobsite. Just for good measure I run through a drive-thru and get everyone coffee. This better pay off. I'm cutting deep into my last 40 bucks. We get to the house at 7:45 and unload our tools. I tell the guys that we aren't going to start until Buddy shows up. He shows at ten after eight. He's jumpy but clean. He talks to the homeowner then unloads the paint and spray rig into the owner's garage. It's at least a day before we will be ready for these but I reckon it's a show for the homeowner, whatever works. He makes a big production of giving the two guys from Friday a fifty dollar bill each, then slips me a C-note. While we work he spends the morning cleaning up every little scrap we drop and eyeballing our every move. I know this is for the homeowner's benefit but it's making the crew nervous. About eleven, I tell him it might be better if he goes to pick up a bucket of fried chicken. He agrees, even gives me props for the idea. After lunch he leaves and we're busting ass. By 4:30 we're prepped, spot primed and ready to start laying on the color. No Buddy. He shows up at 5:15 with a wad of cash, pays us off and says he'll meet us here tomorrow at eight. I'm feeling better about this. I drop the crew off at Homer's. Everybody is cutting up and trash talking. It feels good.

XIII.

The guys are waiting by the Home Depot driveway at 7:45. I don't even have to pull into the parking lot. We get drive-thru coffee and still make the jobsite by ten after eight. Buddy isn't there. At a quarter to nine there's still no Buddy. I decide to step up. I check with the homeowner to make sure which color goes where then assign duties. The young kid will follow me around and knock down any runs as I lay on the base. The "*familia*" will hand paint the trim. It's a midsized suburban house but 6 hours in we appear to be done. We decide to take a late lunch while it dries, come back and see if it needs any touch-up. Buddy is still a no-show. The job looks good. It takes maybe an hour to knock out the touch-ups, clean the spray rig and load out. No Buddy, we wait. It's 4:45 and I have to do something. When I knock on the homeowner's door the wife answers.

"We're all done. Y'all want to check it out?"

"My husband's not home but I'll take a look." she says. She walks around the house then stands by the curb. "It's beautiful," she says, though her expression shows that she isn't sure exactly what to look for.

"Can I use your phone to call my boss? I need to get my guys paid." About then an SUV pulls into the driveway but it isn't Buddy.

"There's Lou, my husband," the wife says. "I'm sure it will be okay to use the phone."

The husband jumps out and strolls around the yard. He's all smiles. "Prettiest house on the block. You guys finished?"

"Yes, sir," I answer. "You can have the leftover paint. There's not much but it might come in handy if you get a scratch."

"Great," he says. "Where's Buddy? I need to get you guys the balance."

"I need to call him. I was hoping to use your phone."

"Sure, come on in. Can I get your guys a beer or something?" At the word "beer" they break into grins.

"Seems like a good plan to me," I say. "Thanks." Lou distributes the beers while I dig out Buddy's business card and dial the phone. His cell goes straight to the message so I take a gamble and dial the office number. A woman answers.

"Is Buddy there?" I ask.

"No!" She is clearly not a happy person.

"I need to reach him. We're finished with this job on Primrose." The line falls silent. "Hello?"

"Shit!" the woman on the phone exclaims. "Just a minute." A few eternal seconds of silence then, "Buddy is indisposed. Do you know where we live?"

I'm beginning to understand that I must be chatting with Buddy's wife. "No," I say, "but I need to get my guys paid and the homeowner is ready to settle up."

"Let me talk to him." I hand the phone to Lou. After a bit Lou hands the phone back to me. "Lou's going to give you the balance. Pay your crew then come to 408 Pocahontas. You know where that is?"

"I've got a map." The phone goes dead. I turn back to Lou. He has a stack of bills.

I walk out of the house with 1400 dollars in my pocket, the most cash I've seen at one time in months, maybe years. The crew is leaning against my car finishing off the six pack. Two couples are standing out front while about a half dozen rug rats cavort on the lawn. The adults don't seem to care. They're admiring the house. One couple and the man from the other couple approach me.

"Nice work," the lone guy says. "Think y'all could make mine look that good? It's the second from the corner down there, the brown one."

"Maybe, if you're not married to brown," I joke. His smile makes me guess he isn't.

"Do you have a card?" he asks.

"Not me but I'll get your number and have the boss give you a call."

"You're not the boss?"

"Nope. I'm just the guy that makes the magic."

"Well, either way, I'd like a bid for you to paint my house."

"Us, too," the woman from the couple says. She hands me a business card for some web design and advertising firm. "You guys do commercial interiors?"

"Paint's paint," I grin. "I've done a lot of interior work." Okay, it was the interior of ships, but still.

"Good, we need our house done, but we're moving our offices to a larger space in a couple of months."

"We'll get back to you." I got the crew loaded up. I'm pretty sure this accidental sales job is going to work into a little bonus when I tell Buddy.

XIV.

I'm sitting in Buddy's kitchen across the table from a tall Hispanic woman. Even with anger oozing out of every pore she's still drop dead gorgeous; liquid brown eyes burn between high cheekbones, voluptuous lips that demand attention and the blackest straightest hair hanging to her shoulders. I'm beginning to get the picture.

"Solicitation, third strike. He's going to be out of circulation for a while." She's biting the words as they leave her mouth. I'm trying to figure out why he would cheat on this goddess while imagining my immediate future swirling down the toilet.

"That sucks," I say. "I got him leads on three more jobs."

"Do them yourself. He'll be in state jail for at least three years. I'm done with him. I'm going out to the west coast and I don't plan to leave a forwarding address."

I count out ten of the 100 dollar bills and slide them across the table. She looks at me as if I have a pair of noses. "I don't want his damn money. As far as I'm concerned his shit is just baggage." She takes one of the bills and shoves the others back toward me. "I tell you what, I just sold you his business, truck, equipment, leads, the whole fucking nine yards. The son of a bitch set me up with power of attorney last time this happened. Dumb ass, serves him right! Let me find the truck title. Here's the fucker's phone. You'll probably find that about half of his contacts are hookers. Want a beer?"

"Sure," I say. I feel like I might have lost consciousness and stumbled into a surreal dream. "Are you sure you want to do this?"

She looks me over, brings a hand up to her hip and drops it back. She looks me dead in the eye until my blood temperature elevates a couple of degrees. "Yeah, you seem like a nice enough guy and I damn sure want to be rid of Buddy."

"You could sell his stuff for a lot of cash," I say.

"Not tonight I couldn't. I'm gone tomorrow." She completes the paperwork, puts his ledgers and Rolodex in a box, gives me the contact info for his phone company and a signed blank check on his bank account. After she drives me to the impound lot to pick up the truck, she follows me to my hotel to drop it off then takes me back to her house to pick up my car.

"Thanks so much, I'm astounded," I say. "There's no way I could make this up to you."

"Sure there is," she says. "Stay the night."

I have no illusions about this going anywhere. I know, for her, it's about revenge. I'm adaptable. I'll do my best to make the revenge as sweet as possible.

WILLOW GARDEN

A 19th century "Dime Novel"

Down in the willow garden

Where me and my love did meet...

That's where I murdered that dear little girl

whose name was Rose Conlee.

-traditional bluegrass ballad

My name is Byron Elliot Conlee, christened for my father, for his father, to five generations. Many men have perished by my hand, more than can be claimed by the most heinous outlaw or the most valiant soldier. You will not, however, find my name among the dime novels or academic testaments of our time. I am but a tool of justice. I am the hangman.

I have looked into the eyes of men preparing to cross the river Styx and I have seen many things. The righteous walk the final steps with dignity and grace. It is the men with dark, evil souls who protest. I have dragged these men, crying like a wounded child, clutching at anything, up the gallows stair.

I once chanced to meet a well known gunfighter. He had delivered the body of a notorious cattle thief to the magistrate and was paid five hundred dollars, tenfold the payment I receive for a single death. We were in the local saloon one evening. When he discovered my occupation, we had occasion to discuss men of honor. He claimed they never cry for mercy when faced with death. "These ghosts ride with you throughout your days." The notches on the black walnut handle of his revolver numbered seventeen. I countered that I had no such ghosts. I am only an agent in a legal system bringing civilized society to the frontier, an agent of man's law and of God's law. My own mother gave her life to this frontier. She believed a civilized society was God's will. I plan to prove her right. I am not the judge. I am but a means.

The gunfighter professed to know the souls of men. "As I rode into this town," he stated, "mothers pulled their children indoors, men turned their faces away and I was told I was not welcome at the inn. Even the women of the bordello had no bed for me. I was forced to sleep in the livery with my mount. Let me demonstrate the fickleness of the human character." He called the bartender over, purchased a bottle of top shelf Kentucky bourbon and loudly proclaimed, "Drinks all around until this bottle is dry." Not one patron refused his drink. "I have ghosts," he said. "You have them as well. It is only honor that is in short supply."

It was some years before I met that man again. Were it not for our previous encounter I must wonder if he would have climbed the stairs in such a regal manner, asking for no hood, only that he end his life looking into the setting sun. His last wish was that I be given his revolver. At the time of his passing the walnut grip had twenty-three notches and I received my initial ghost.

The sunlight was illuminating the low crests of the surrounding hills. In this lush valley, however, a thick mist sat heavily on the laconic river. We had searched most of the night, my father and I, accompanied by the sheriff and several town folk. She had not returned by the fall of night. Her place at the supper table had not been visited. By the ten o'clock hour we were searching. The night had passed slowly with no results. The dawning of the day allowed a visual benefit but deepened our concern. I was the unfortunate soul to spot the whiteness tangled on the riverbank. I scrambled through the brush with my heart thumping my throat. As I approached, my body slowed as the brambles tore at my legs. My hands were bloodied by branches. I found myself knee-deep in the black water. She floated in the mire, her long black hair tangled in the gnarled roots of a bald cypress. Her wide eyes stared blankly into the unknown. Her white cotton dress hung on her shoulders, ripped wide from the neckline to the knees. A pearl handled dagger was buried deep in her breast. The agony overcame me and I fell to my knees in the river clutching her cold, stiff body. My precious Rose, my baby sister, my friend and confidant lie cold and gray in the chilling river. Anger welled in me beyond my physical capacity to contain it for I knew well the owner of the lethal knife. So often I had pleaded with her not to consort with this miscreant. The gaudily tooled dagger was the property of Earl Knox, the chosen beau of my dear sister.

"The man is dangerous," I tried to explain not a fortnight ago. "He possesses an illness of mind and partakes of the fermented grape with great frequency."

"He loves me truly. He told me as much," She pleaded.

"I suppose those are the marks of love settled on your wrists like violet shackles. And why is it you wear your veil though it is not the Sabbath? Do you think me blind, sweet sister? I fear for your safety!"

"It is merely his lust that drives him. Once we wed he will settle into a temperate life. He has great wealth. He promises a balcony overlooking the ocean and servants to prepare my meals."

"Oh my poor dazzled sister, he has no money. The wealth of which he speaks is that of his father. Once he leaves the fold his fortune will dry up like spit on a summer street. What will be your fate then?"

"You are a vicious brother! I do not believe you! You would prefer that I shrivel and perish on this dusty prairie like my namesake, like our dear mother."

"There are many strong, honorable men in this town. You are a beautiful young flower. Is there no real man here for you?"

"They are dusty and course like this town!"

"So you prefer this effeminate, lace encrusted fool who wishes to own you? I must warn you, the wine he thirsts for is evil!"

"And you, dear brother, I know you imbibe in the pleasures of rye whiskey."

"That is so, but the clear liquor does not alter the sensibilities."

"So you say, but wine is the blood of Christ."

"When sanctified by the Church! Many things of God, when used in a sacrilegious manner, are but tools of the Devil. I have seen men drunk on the nectar of the grape lust for the loins of other men. That, my sweet sister, is against God and man. Your prissy beau, with his lace trimmed blouse and snug breeches, frankly, I do not understand your fascination."

"No, my brother, I suppose not, for you are as course as this outpost of civilization we inhabit."

"Please, sweet Rose, let us not quarrel. You are all I know of love and beauty and I will be beside you forever. I only ask that you not rush blindly toward this Earl Knox. I am afraid he may have a perverse plan for you. I do not want to see you disgraced."

The conversation played through my mind as I wrapped her cold, wet body in my waistcoat. My father and I transported her to the waiting buckboard, the lines in his face deepening with each step. I had but one goal at that time and it was vengeance.

The scoundrel awaited us at his father's estate. He was contrite as the sheriff bound him for transport. He sneered and taunted us with the statement of his father. "Worry not, my fair-haired son, for the power of wealth shall set you free."

I waited as he fretted in his iron cage. I visited him regularly. "You were the chosen of my dear sister," I told him. "Fear not, I will stand beside you throughout this ordeal." I fixed my eyes upon him as I watched the color drain from his features.

The forthcoming arrival of the circuit judge was postponed as fall degenerated into a grizzly winter. I had ample occasion to visit young Earl Knox. Through my friendship with the sheriff, bail was denied. Though the Knox family wealth was great, our township was one of few administered by men of integrity. Useless attempts were made to bribe the sheriff and the magistrate. The Knox family hired mercenaries to orchestrate a jail break. Three men fell to the weapons of the constabulary. Two of them perished and the unfortunate survivor is but a shell of a man. Earl Knox remained a prisoner.

On the eve of the winter Solstice I received a communiqué from a gentleman in St. Louis. It had come to his attention, through means not revealed to me, that I was in possession of a revolver formerly owned by a famous gunfighter. He was prepared to pay me six thousand dollars for the weapon. Though tempted by his offer, I could not leave my objective unfinished. I responded that I would consider his offer but travel through the territory at this time would be ill advised.

Through the course of the winter I called on Earl Knox regularly, pleasing his palette with rare steak, fine mutton and wines of his choosing. It was my intention to gain a rapport with him for I had an enigma gnawing at my soul. I wanted, no, required an explanation. Why? I was aware that his testimony in court would be slanted. Before I took his life it was imperative that I discern his motivation.

The day came, as I knew it would, when he called me into his confidence. "Come to speak with me after the sheriff retires. We have many things to discuss." Time attained the consistency of blackstrap molasses as I anticipated the setting of the sun. From the inn, I acquired a medium rare rib eye steak complete with a bowl of fresh snow peas. I resisted the temptation to spit on the dinner plate. Offering the meal to Earl Knox, I requested of him the reason for my visit. He gushed over my offering and asked me to sit with him as he masticated the rib eye. Upon completion of the meal he turned to me. "You are aware, of course, that my father has great wealth. He is a powerful man and yet he has approached the magistrate, the sheriff and the circuit judge. He has had no success in gaining my freedom. You have been unusually and unnecessarily kind to me. I have a discreet proposal for you."

"You know why I have lingered by your side. I want the true reason for you ending the life of my precious sister. I claim no friendship or affection for you. My goal is only that knowledge. Any consideration that you receive from me will, of necessity, require that knowledge."

Earl Knox considered my request briefly. "I have had a long time to ponder that while I endured my incarceration here. Though my mind was confused at the time, I feel I can explain the justification as I saw it. First, however, I would like to propose monetary compensation in return for you arranging my escape. You are my final contingency. If you would consider assisting with my freedom, what would be my cost?"

"I would think the amount would be obvious. The method of payment would need to be arranged."

"You say the amount should be obvious and yet nothing you have said answers the query. What would be your compensation?"

"Thirty pieces of silver, thirty silver dollars would ensure my cooperation. I will need your confession as to your motivation for the bloody murder of my sister as well. Consider these demands and I will arrange for a method of payment." As I parted his company he reclined on his bunk, fingers entwined behind his head, and bid me adieu.

The evening brought no rest as I pondered the greed and dishonor eating my soul away. Was I, as my dear sister stated, a course and ruthless man? Could I experience a reformation? Did it matter? As the sun lightened the eastern horizon these questions remained unanswered and sleep had not come. I allowed a week to pass before revisiting Earl Knox. It was a week of torment and introspection but a solution was forming in my mind.

I arrived at the jail just before sunset as plans such as mine should never see the light of day. I fought back the disgust upon confronting Earl Knox. I presented him with a silk kerchief belonging to my sister Rose. It had been doused with her chosen perfume. I cringed as the lout held it to his face. Tears welled in his eyes.

"Wrap the thirty pieces of silver in the kerchief and have your agent leave it under the willow tree where you assassinated my sister. Now I will hear your confession, then I will explain my plan for your earthly salvation. I cannot, nor would I, do anything about the fires of Hell that await you in the afterlife."

Earl Knox sat on his bunk and pondered a moment as if he were sitting around a campfire preparing to spin a yarn. " Byron, it was never my intention to kill Rose. She was a lovely maiden and I planned to make her my wife. Sitting in the willow garden by the river, her beauty and precociousness overcame me and lust boiled in my loins. I asked her if she would share a bottle of burgundy wine with me, hoping it would loosen the laces of her corset. She refused me as she had many times before. She said that our union should be sanctified by God. She then teased me with stories of how she was rubbing cream on her skin and studying the art of lovemaking by talking to older women with successful marriages. My passions were inflamed. I had to get her to drink of the grape so that she would not resist me. I drew her to me and we began kissing. As she began to push away, I clutched her throat and squeezed until she fainted. As she slept, I tried to pour the wine down her throat. She awoke with a start accusing me of trying to poison her. She began screaming like a banshee that her brother was right, I was a pervert. She insisted that I take her home. When I refused she became a shrew such as I have never known, lunging at me with teeth bared and nails at the ready. I feared for my safety. I had no choice but to defend myself with the dagger hanging from my belt. Do you see? It was my life or hers."

"You took her life for your foibles?" I asked. "And I suppose you violated her as she lay dying?"

"She was quite deceased when I enjoyed her pleasures," he bragged.

The room was spinning. I forced my hands to grip the iron bars to keep them from ripping him apart. I stepped out of the cell onto the street to regain my composure. It was difficult to breathe. I stood as a wooden Indian would on the porch of the jailhouse for what seemed like an eternity. It was hard to remember my promise to myself but new ideas were forming in my mind. After I finally relaxed I reentered the jail.

"I have no reason to spare you from the gallows save my honor," I stated. "However, a promise is a promise. You will need to follow my instructions to the letter and you will survive your hanging. When I measure you for the rope I will give you enough to allow your feet to touch the ground. It is imperative that you stand erect as the trap is opened. As you know we enclose the area below the gallows in canvas so as not to shock the women and children attending the event. I will have a buckboard with a coffin on it placed underneath. The coffin will be loaded with rocks approximating your weight. After I pull the trap, I will go below and cut you free placing you among the rocks. I will put two small nails in the coffin lid. I have agreed to transport the body to the undertaker as he has family coming into town to participate in the festivities and he wishes to take them out for a meal afterwards. Once I give you the signal you can force your way out of the coffin and go free. Remember to securely nail down the lid. You will need to leave the territory and assume a new identity. If fortune smiles on us no one will know. Otherwise, you should at least have several hours head start. This all depends on my stipend being delivered as per my demand."

"Have no doubt you will be rewarded," Earl Knox assured me.

"Remember, I can make the gallows quick and efficient or I can assure a slow and painful death." I fixed him in my gaze and spun on my boot heel, exiting without further conversation. I made no further contact with Earl Knox prior to his scheduled day of execution.

As the day of execution approached, I watched my father sink deeper and deeper into the void. He no longer spoke nor attended to his hardware and mercantile operation. I did what I could to keep his business open as it helped to alleviate the dread and shame my future held. The sunset of my father's life was at hand. I had watched him fade since the untimely death of his wife. With his daughter buried it was as if his soul had vacated his body, leaving only a shell. For him, for God, it was my duty to deliver Earl Knox to the fires of Hell.

On the day of reckoning I arose before the sun, holstered the gunfighter's prized weapon, packed a saddlebag and headed for the river where my sister had met her fate. As I approached the blood stained boulder I saw the lily white kerchief bundled on the rock. I untied it and counted out the thirty pieces of silver. After sitting on the boulder contemplating the trading of justice for personal gain, I took the coins to the river and skipped them one by one across the calm water as would an innocent child with smooth, flat stones. I tucked the kerchief into my breast pocket and mounted my horse, turning back toward town.

Upon reaching the jail I encountered the padre in contact with the accused. I asked for a moment with Earl Knox. The priest seemed relieved to relinquish the attentions of the prisoner. The father met my eyes with a look of thanks. Upon the departure of the priest I informed Earl Knox that the agreed payment had not been found.

"That is impossible!" He screamed. "My own father was to have placed it there!"

"How is it to finally realize your monetary worth?" I mocked.

"Bring my father to me. There must be some mistake."

"The time is nigh. We have but minutes."

"Please, I beg of you. I have my own money hidden. I will pay you double if you will spare me!"

"And how do you propose to make this happen?"

"Spare me and I will bring you a generous bag of gold. I will meet you at the rock one hour after the scheduled hanging, on my honor."

"Your honor? I have seen no evidence of honor! I should slice you open and let you watch your entrails spill before you! I will, however, give you this last opportunity. If you fail I will spend my life tracking you down. Your death will be slow and painful and all time before it will be filled with fear and apprehension. As God is my witness, I will prevail!"

"Yes, certainly, thank you my friend."

"You will survive your hanging. I am not your friend." I tied his hands behind his waist. "Would you care for a blindfold?" I asked.

"I see no need for one."

I led him to the gallows. The boisterous crowd grew quiet as we climbed the gallows stair. I placed the noose around his neck. He stood solemn without speaking. The padre spoke a brief prayer over him and descended from the platform. As I pulled the lever the silent crowd gasped in unison followed by a raucous cheer. I left the platform taking the receding steps slowly. Under the gallows I found Earl Knox suspended from the noose, his toes touching the ground, the rope snug around his throat. His face was inflamed as he gasped for air. I pulled his pearl handled dagger from my belt and flashed it before his eyes. I grabbed the strap cinching his hands and pulled down, tightening the noose. I stood behind him pressing my body firmly against his. I wrapped my free arm around his shoulder holding the shiny knife against his throat just below the noose.

"My blood and my being are screaming for vengeance. Even my loins want you to feel the degradation experienced by my sister. My love! Not yours!" I hissed, acknowledging the swelling pressing against his buttocks. "It is only my honor that frees you." I took the dagger from his throat and sliced through the rope above the knot. I picked him up and threw him forcefully into the rock filled coffin. I finally cut the strap from his wrist. As tears streamed from his eyes, I tacked the coffin lid closed. Taking my seat on the buckboard I drove to the undertaker's barn and pulled into the shadows where my mount waited. I pounded on the coffin, mounted my steed and rode toward the river.

I am sitting on the rock speaking face to face with the ghosts residing in the barrel of the gunfighter's revolver. They are explaining to me about blood and honor. I have sold my honor for knowledge. I am told by these ghosts that my only hope to reconnect with my sister is to mix our blood on this rock where she died. Just as these apparitions are about to assist me with this magical union, I hear a rustling in the brush. I look up to see my nemesis, Earl Knox, holding a leather pouch. I holster the haunted weapon and take the bag.

"You should have pulled the trigger," Earl Knox taunts. "You can never return to your home. You are now as much of an outlaw as I am."

"I should have let you hang. We would both be free."

"I am as free as a bird. Only your honor binds you in shame."

I pull the pistol from my holster. The first shot finds his groin, doubling him over.

"Your promise!" He screams.

"My promise was fulfilled when you survived the noose!" I exclaim. I pull the white kerchief from my shirt to place under my nose, inhaling the last faint hint of my sister, Rose. Upon realization, Earl Knox attempts to lunge at me. The second shot finds his chest, knocking him off his feet and into the river. Although the third shot misses, the fourth removes his flawless face from the front of his head. As Earl Knox joins the silver coins, I use the pearl handled dagger to carve another notch into the revolver. The ghosts are silenced. I holster the weapon, mount my horse and begin the journey to St. Louis.

THE

AMERICANA

TRILOGY

HIDING IN PLAIN SIGHT

The truck saw its heyday at the peak of the American steel industry, the exact middle of the twentieth century; one of the last "five window" Chevys, one of the last with vacuum operated wipers, one of the last with a starter button. Tommy fully expected it to be his one day. After all, it was passed down from his mother's father to his dad so naturally, Tommy being the oldest, well it seemed obvious. Even though the beast had seen over a dozen years of service it still maintained its roadworthiness. Thanks to Poppa Seamus the corrosive coastal air hadn't assaulted the steel panels of the truck's body. Between the toxic emissions of the giant Dow Chemical company and the salty coastal breeze, few vehicles made it much past five years old before rocker panels and fenders were rusted through. When Poppa Seamus changed the oil ritually at the beginning of every season he sprayed the used oil over the vehicle like an extra coat of paint. He never washed it. It made for a slimy, dirty truck but it didn't rust. Tommy's dad inherited the vehicle after hurricane Carla devastated the Texas coast. The family moved out to the country, as his dad called it, though you could still smell the chlorine and sulfur from the chemical plant when the wind blew from the south.

Tommy's dad had the spirit of an entrepreneur. In the wake of Carla, he helped with the cleanup efforts, though his motives were less than altruistic. It takes a large number of boards and posts to subdivide a 30 acre pasture into the corrals and paddocks necessary for a successful horse breeding operation. In addition, the long pilings that supported elevated housing on the beach could supply framing material for a sturdy stable. Tommy's dad hooked the old '56 Ford station wagon to a sixteen foot trailer and headed for the coastline as soon as the storm surge receded. His buddy, Steve, who owned an auto salvage yard just out of the flood plain, brought a wrecker to help. He also brought his son, Billy, who was only two years older than Tommy. Tommy had to stay home and sulk. Even Tommy's mom was allowed to help with the project. Since Tommy was as strong as a kid much older than eight it just didn't seem fair.

On the third trip across the Intracoastal waterway, Tommy's dad began a specific search for the heavy timbers. Though knocked down like dominoes by the raging hurricane, many were still solidly imbedded in the soggy sand. Spotting three of the poles entangled with other debris, Steve hooked the winch cable to one. Tommy's dad grabbed a nearby scrap of 2 by 4 to use as a lever. The guttural rumble of the wrecker's engine revving as the cable retracted drowned out the ominous warning. Tommy's dad felt the fiery sting in his ankles and calf before he saw the diamondback rattlesnakes curling around his feet. He jumped straight up and hit the ground running, tripping and falling into the debris adding several abrasions and punctures to the growing list of injuries. The snakes slithered away to parts unknown as the humans jumped on or in the wrecker.

"There's a snakebite kit in the glove compartment," Steve said as he put the wrecker in granny gear and dragged the one pole free of the snake pit. he cautiously loosened the cable and retracted it with the winch. He told Billy to hold on in the truck bed and he returned to the driver's seat. Tommy's mom had already removed her husband's shoes and ripped both pants legs to the knee with the razor blade from the snake bite kit. She sliced across the punctures and used the rubber suction to draw out venom contaminated blood.

"There's too many bites, four at least!" She cried as she watched the red hot streaks inching up his legs. "We have to get to the hospital, fast!"

Steve jammed the wrecker in gear and bounced across the dunes until he found a semblance of a road. He floored it. Tommy's dad was having trouble breathing, red and purple splotches covered his skin and he'd already vomited twice.

"Please hurry!" Tommy's mom screamed.

"I'm giving her all she's got." Steve replied. The needle on the speedometer bounced around 80 miles per hour.

Dow Chemical Company owned Freeport Community Hospital. Since the chemical plants were spread all over the salt grass prairie the hospital had plenty of experience with snake bites. When Steve skidded the wrecker into the emergency drive, Tommy's dad was unconscious and his breathing was shallow.

"Rattlesnakes, at least four of them!" Tommy's mom screamed. She still sucked the contaminated blood from the punctures. Her hands and clothes were covered in the sticky substance.

"We'll take it from here. Are you sure it was rattlesnakes?" The head trauma nurse asked.

"Diamondbacks, big ones," Steve said.

"He has at least four bites," Tommy's mom reiterated.

"Who's his doctor?" The nurse asked.

"Berryman"

"He's out today but we can get the staff doctor here for now. We need to get him on antivenin. Do you know if he's allergic?"

"I don't know. It's never come up."

"We're going to have to risk it. He has a lot of poison in him."

"Do what you have to do. Please hurry!"

"If he's allergic to the serum he'll die."

"If you don't give him the serum?"

"He'll die, painfully." The doctor held her gaze.

'Help him if you can." A sense of resignation took the urgency from her voice. She collapsed into a nearby chair. "Can I stay with him?"

"Of course." The doctor shifted his gaze to Steve who was waiting nearby. Are you family?"

"A friend," Steve muttered.

"You will need to wait out front." The doctor administered the antivenin. As the minutes ticked by, Tommy's dad began breathing in a regular pattern and the blotches on his skin faded. Minutes became hours. Tommy's mom continued to fidget as hospital personnel cleaned and dressed the superficial wounds. Steve and Billy sat in the waiting room perusing various outdated magazines.

"Water," Tommy's dad whispered as Tommy's mom was staring out the window. She rushed to his bed and took his hand.

"Thirsty --- something to drink --- please?" There was desperation in his voice.

"Let me get you something. How do you feel?" Tommy's mom asked.

"I'm burning - thirsty, please."

Tommy's mom rushed out to find the nurse.

"No liquids," The nurse said.

"What!" Tommy's mom barked, livid.

"Let me see what I can do." The nurse left, returning momentarily with a small paper cup of ice chips. "Give him these, sparingly," she said. "He may not be able to hold them down."

"This is all you can have," Tommy's mom apologized, placing a bit of ice on her husband's tongue. He devoured them. The more coherent he became, the more pain he experienced. Tommy's mom called for the doctor. After a brief examination, he spoke directly to Tommy's dad.

"You had a close call but it you'll pull through. We'll keep an eye on you for about 48 hours. When you get a little stronger we'll give you some antibiotics and a tetanus shot," the doctor reassured. "In the meantime get some rest. I can give you a shot for pain. It'll make you sleepy.

"Can I have something to drink?" Tommy's dad asked.

"I'll have the nurse bring you some tea but go easy on it. You may experience some nausea."

"My sister has the kids," Tommy's mom explained to her husband. "I'm going to stay with you. Steve's here. I'll tell him to go on home."

The doctor left. Tommy's mom threw herself on her husband and wept. "God, you scared me! I didn't know. I thought I'd lost you."Her body shook with emotion. He felt her hot tears running down his neck.

"I'll to be okay," he said. "What a mess, huh?"

"Yeah, a mess. I love you so much."

Tommy's dad stayed in the hospital for four days due to a minor reaction to one of the antibiotics. The day after he was released he spent the morning convincing his wife that they should return to the beach and pick up the car and trailer. They piled all three kids and two adults into the little Studebaker Lark that Tommy's dad drove to work. When they crossed the bridge over the Intracoastal Canal the view from the top looked like a bombing range, splintered houses, overturned boats and cars, devastation to the horizon in both directions down the coast. When they reached the haunted area from where they'd evacuated only five days before, there was no sign of the car or trailer. They'd been stolen or mistakenly salvaged. There was nothing to do but drive back home. The trip was long and quiet. Tommy's dad called the county sheriff and reported the car stolen. He'd scabbed the trailer together from salvaged purlin and old mobile home axles. Since he'd never registered it he elected not to mention it to the constabulary.

Tommy's dad flopped down in his recliner. Tommy's mom started dinner. Tommy's brother and sister went to their rooms and lost themselves in their respective toy boxes. That left Tommy to sit in the thick silence and hope for a miracle. After dinner everybody went to bed early. Tommy sweated in the late summer dusk and listened to his parents whisper in the next room. He couldn't decipher the sentences but an occasional sob from his mother cut into him.

The next morning Tommy awoke to the rusty Studebaker sputtering down the driveway. In the kitchen, he found his mother with her head in her hands staring into her coffee cup.

"Where's Dad going?" Tommy asked.

"Work."

"Already?"

"That's what I asked, but you know him."

Tommy did know him and he wasn't surprised. "He'll be fine," Tommy reassured her.

"I know." She got up and put her coffee cup in the sink. "We have chores." She grabbed the bucket of last night's table scraps from under the counter and exited through the back door. Tommy followed.

About noon the phone rang, unusual as they were on a party line. The widow Mrs. Parsons usually kept the line tied up from morning until well into the afternoon. If you picked up and asked to use it you had better have a good reason and you had better be ready to explain that reason in great detail to the widow Mrs. Parsons. If you weren't an adult you could just forget it. So when the phone rang in the middle of the day Tommy's mom said, "Mrs. Parsons must have keeled over dead," and then, "Oh, my! I didn't say that!" Tommy burst out laughing as his mom reached for the phone.

"Hello."

"Hi Mom. --- I can't, Mom, I'd love to but our wagon was stolen. --- While J.D. was in the hospital. --- the Studebaker, but J.D. took it to work. --- Yeah, already. He'd go crazy if he had to sit still for even a minute. --- No but tell me about it. --- that silver blue that Buick came out with last year? --- sounds pretty. I've never heard of an F-85. --- Oh my, J.D. would never buy any new model. He wants them to work the bugs out first. In fact, the only new car we ever owned was that Special we bought right after we got married. --- since it's an automatic you can drive it to the bowling alley so me or Lois won't have to pick you up. --- Can you just give me a minute! --- I've got to go, Mom, Mrs. Parsons *needs* the line. Call me this evening, okay? --- Bye."

Saturday was an odd one. The storm had passed but a change lay in its wake. Tommy wondered if things would ever get back to normal. Summer Saturdays were usually large celebrations with groups of friends and family coming over to sit under the sprawling oak tree enjoying J.D.'s award-winning barbeque and drinking copious quantities of beer. This Saturday no one came. Tommy followed his dad around helping with minor repairs on various fences and outbuildings. The burn pile grew larger with downed limbs and storm debris but no flame gave life to the cold structure.

Tommy was dragging a burlap feed bag around the back yard picking up little pieces of trash in preparation for a good mowing when he heard vehicles advancing, the tires crunching on the oyster shell driveway. Tommy ran around front as Poppa Seamus pulled the dirty old Chevy pickup into the parking area. He was followed by a woman in a brand new car, a sporty model with jaunty lines and chrome accents driven by a woman in a colorful scarf, red lipstick and oversized dark shades. It took Tommy a few seconds to register that the woman was his Granny Leah. Tommy's mom came out on the porch and , upon seeing her mother, ran to embrace the tiny woman. Tommy's dad came around the other end of the house holding a roofing hatchet which he buried into a fence post and extended a hand to Poppa Seamus. After formalities, the family gathered around the sleek Oldsmobile. Poppa Seamus presided over the crowd, explaining the marvel of technology that shone before them. "This baby has power steering, power brakes , an aluminum block V-8 and air conditioning. The announcement of each option brought a gasp or swoon from the collective except Tommy's dad who felt this was a list of untested systems destined to fail and cause great expense. After every detail of the miracle car was examined and explained Poppa Seamus turned to Tommy's dad. He fished a set of keys from the pocket of his striped overalls and handed them over.

"I won't be needing this truck anymore. I thought with this spread you have maybe you could use it,"

Tommy's dad seemed to have trouble comprehending the situation. It was no secret that he and Poppa Seamus rarely saw eye to eye. Not one to "look a gift horse in the mouth" as he would often say, J.D. graciously accepted.

"Thanks." He said. "Would ya'll like to stay for dinner?"

"I told Leah I would take her out to dinner," Poppa Seamus said. "Bodeckers has reopened. They have new windows made from some kind of unbreakable plastic. We thought we would go see what that's like. Why don't ya'll join us?"

"I don't care about the windows but if they still have that amazing cocktail sauce and oysters on the half shell, count me in. Come on in and give us a few minutes to get ready," Tommy's dad said.

Granny Leah got quiet. She stepped inside but never smiled or took off her scarf or shades. It was unusual for her to not interact with her grandchildren. Tommy had never seen her dressed up or wearing make-up either. she looked like the women at the funeral of his other grandmother when he was five, She seemed, at that moment, just as sad.

Bodeckers did not suffer much from the flood. It was a big metal building with a kitchen on one end and a bar on the other. In between was a huge dining area with long lines of picnic tables butted end to end. The overhead doors on both sides were full of windows but were only closed during inclement weather. Skinny waitresses hustled steaming platters of seafood from the kitchen and ice cold trays of longnecks from the bar. It was a boisterous atmosphere. Tommy's dad felt at home here. Dusk brought out the neon of the beer signs and the environment took on a glassy sheen.

Tommy had to ask. "Granny Leah, why are you still wearing those big ole shades? It's dark outside."

"I'm pretending to be a famous movie star, incognito," she replied.

"What's incognito?" Tommy asked.

"It's like hiding in plain sight."

Tommy thought about this for a minute but the tone in her reply prevented him from asking any more questions,.

Tommy and his little brother were allowed to ride home in the bed of the pickup. The evening air buffeting around them was exhilarating. Once home they bounded out of the truck bed with no thought of coming in for the night. It was not, however, their choice as they soon discovered.

Tommy's mom seemed reserved as she carried his sleeping sister into the house, mumbling something about an elaborate apology.

"It's still not right," Tommy's dad said. He sat down on the front stoop and finished his cigarette. Tommy sat beside him.

"See those stars above the high branch on that pecan tree? Do you know what those are?" Tommy's dad asked.

"The big dipper," Tommy stated.

"You sure? Look over there," Tommy's dad pointed.

Tommy realized his dad was pointing at the big dipper.

"Oops, must be the little one,"

"Yep, part of it. You can't see everything. Some parts are hidden,"

The next morning the family ate the traditional multi-course Sunday breakfast. Instead of sprawling over the living room furniture as usual, Tommy's dad herded everyone outside with a washcloth each. He brought out the container of dish detergent and a five gallon bucket. After pulling the pickup to the center of the front yard, they made a family project of removing the years of oily grime from the truck. It took a couple of hours but there was a good looking truck under all the slime.

"Tommy and I are going to put the finishing touches on it," Tommy's dad announced, releasing the rest of the family from the soggy servitude. Tommy's dad rinsed out two of the washrags and refilled the bucket with clean water. "Honey, can you bring me the Turtle Wax from under the sink?" Tommy's dad asked his wife.

Tommy and his dad spent most of the afternoon polishing, waxing and buffing the truck until it sparkled like a new dime and there wasn't a clean towel in the house.

The truck served well and when the horse breeding operation began showing a profit Tommy's mom and dad left one morning in the old Studebaker. They came home a few hours later in an almost new Ford Ranch Wagon complete with those fancy wood-grained decals on the side. His mother was ecstatic.

Over the next couple of years the horse business prospered and Tommy's dad began picking up an occasional piece of farm equipment. Although he had a good paying construction job as a welding contractor, he knew construction was a fickle business.

It must have been fifth grade. Tommy had Mrs. Donaldson's class. The crusty old crone had no understanding or tolerance for his sense of humor or creative needs. She taught the driest facts from rote and memorization. Tommy had never felt such a bitter dislike for a teacher. Ambivalence maybe, but Mrs. Donaldson rubbed his every nerve raw. He'd spent the day trying unsuccessfully to memorize pointless dates of pointless battles in pointless wars. The wind howled when he stepped off the school bus stinging his face with damp crystals. He still had a quarter mile to walk to get home. His brother seemed oblivious to the cold. His little sister plopped down on her book bag and refused to walk. Usually if the weather was bad , their mother picked them up in the car. Not today. Tommy persuaded his little sister to accompany them by promising to carry her books. She looked like she might break into tears at any minute. The Christmas break had ended and it seemed like eons until the next holiday.

The kids stepped into the warm house and began shedding coats and bags. They huddled around the space heater until feeling returned to their fingers. Once warm they realized no mom had greeted their arrival. There was, however, a lot of noise coming from the back of the house. Tommy went to his room and saw his mother carelessly tossing his clothes and books into a large wooden crate.

"Mom?"

She startled and wiped her face before turning.

"What are you doing?" Tommy asked the frazzled woman.

"You're going to have to room with your brother for a while. Granny Leah is going to stay with us. She needs your room for now. Can you help me with your stuff?"

"Sure. I'll get it all. Just relax." Partly Tommy saw his mother was teetering on the brink of something and partly he didn't want anyone, especially his mom, messing with his stuff. Tommy wasn't happy with the arrangement but he knew it was inevitable. His brother, on the other hand began marking his territory.

That evening, as soon as his dad walked in the door, his mom left. It took two hours of strained quiet and bologna sandwiches before his mom returned. As his mom drove up she honked the horn and his dad went out to meet her. Tommy tried to see out but by that time it was dark and the cold. Wet wind absorbed any light from the house.

They brought Granny through the door in a wheelchair. Her left arm was in a cast and the right side of her face was swollen and blue. She had several stitches in a cut above her eye.

"What happened.? Tommy gasped.

Granny Leah managed to stand but not straighten up. "I fell down the steps behind the house, rolled all the way to the creek bank."

Tommy had fished that creek many times. It seemed strange that she could be hurt that badly rolling down the grassy leaf-covered embankment. She was old, though, maybe she was just brittle.

"Sit back down," Tommy's mom instructed Granny Leah. "I'll take you to your room."

"I can just sleep on the couch. I don't want to put anyone out."

"Don't be silly. This is your home now."

"I'll be up in no time."

"I know but it's not safe to go back."

"We'll see."

Tommy felt something awkward in the arrangement. He really didn't want to give up his room permanently.

Texas winters are short in days but long in hours, dreary and gray with a penetrating dampness driven by incessant wind. Occasionally a piercing bright, crisp day will tease the senses before slapping faces with the dark frosty rag of the season. Slowly Granny Leah recovered until only a white hair of a scar hovered above her eye. The cast came off. The arm regained its strength, but she never stood quite as tall. Soon she was spending time in the kitchen creating the most delicious baked goods. Poppa Seamus hadn't come to visit, at least not while Tommy was home.

One of those bright Spring teasers happened on a Saturday. The outdoors called anyone with a child's heart. Tommy was helping his dad lube and service the seeder in preparation for planting a field of alfalfa. The dogs laying under the nearby oak tree jumped up to announce the imminent arrival of a visitor. The Olds F-85 crunched up the driveway covered in dust and slime. Tommy's dad moved quickly. He met Poppa Seamus at the door of the car before the brake was set. Tommy couldn't hear the conversation but no one was smiling or shaking hands. Poppa Seamus started to open the door to get out but Tommy's dad threw his hip against it and placed his hand on the door. He grabbed the door with both hands and flexed the muscles in his forearm. Tommy was glad he wasn't in that grip. He fully expected to see the door crush like a tin can. Poppa Seamus started the Olds and backed away. As he·turned back down the driveway he slung a bit of oyster shell onto the lawn. Tommy's dad just shook his head and went inside. Tommy finished greasing the equipment the best he knew how.

Tommy entered the house to find his dad sitting at the kitchen table sipping a Lone Star. Tommy's mom stood outside of what used to be his room talking to the door.

"He didn't know. He was just trying to protect you. --- He didn't know if Dad had been drinking or not. --- No, you need to stay here.

You can call him later. --- Please mom. We'll talk after dinner. Just try to relax.

Tommy's mom made fried chicken, the supper meal she made for big family events or Sunday spreads. When the table was set Tommy's mom went to retrieve Granny Leah from the back of the house. Dinner conversation was non-existent until Granny Leah spoke up.

"I'm not a kid you know. I can take care of myself!" No one else spoke.

"He's really sweet when he's not drinking!" No one replied. "Well, somebody say something."

Tommy's dad scooted his chair back. He took a swallow of his Lone Star and stuck a toothpick in his teeth. "You were nearly killed," he said. "But you're right. We don't own you. You have a history with him, good, bad or otherwise, I can't tell you what to do."

"I need to go home"

"Please, Mom, you know you're welcome here!" Tommy's mom said. Her eyes looked wet.

"I know sweetie but my place is with him. That's what God intended."

Tommy's dad snorted and sprang from the table, thrusting his empty bottle into the garbage can. He hurried through the back letting the screen door slam behind him.

"What got into him?" Granny Leah asked.

"He don't believe in God's plan and he gets frustrated with those who do. Just let him be. He gets over it," Tommy's mom explained.

Tommy's mom and Granny Leah cleared the table and washed the dishes together. After dinner, while everyone was watching TV, Granny Leah took the phone and stretched it into the kitchen. A few minutes later she came back. "He's coming to pick me up in the morning. He doesn't want any trouble. Neither do I."

"Fine. No problem," Tommy's dad stated.

Sunday morning the greasy F-85 rolled up just after breakfast. Tommy's dad decided it was time to feed the livestock. It didn't take long for Granny Leah to load her few items in the car. She gave her husband a hug and he kissed her gently on the forehead as if she were fragile. He then went around and opened the passenger door for her. They pulled away slowly.

Tommy's dad came in from his chores and looked at Tommy with a curious stare. "Hold out your hands," he told Tommy, showing what he wanted, stiff, palms down. Tommy obeyed. "Pretty stable I'd say." Tommy's dad smiled. "It's about time I start teaching you what I know about metalworking. He lead Tommy outside and rolled out the acetylene cutting torch. He showed Tommy the gauges on the tanks and explained how they should read, then the adjustments on the torch. "This is a little more individual depending on the metal and how fast and how clean you want to cut," he said. This is the part you have to get the feel for yourself." After a brief rundown Tommy's dad rolled the rig over next to the Chevy pickup. He fired up the torch.

"If you're just doing demolition," he said, "you want to start high and work down so you don't burn yourself with the hot slag. Put these on." He handed Tommy a pair of very dark shades. "Watch while I get you started, then I'll turn it over to you."

Tommy watched as his dad placed the torch near the top of the truck's front fender. As the flame turned toward the metal a spot on the surface immediately turned into a pool of glowing orange liquid. Tommy's dad pulled the oxygen trigger and a nickel sized hole exploded through the fender. Sliding the torch along a few centimeters from the metal a clean gash began forming. He handed the torch to Tommy. Tommy heated the metal at the edge of the gash and pulled the lever. Slag splattered in several directions but a large chunk fell on the ground sizzling in the grass and causing the blades to shrivel and burst into flames.

"Tilt the torch," Tommy's dad instructed. The metal separated in a clean straight line. The heat and aggressiveness of the flame gave Tommy a feeling of power. After a little more instruction, mostly about planning ahead to when the piece separates, Tommy's dad pulled up a lawn chair. When the fender hit the ground he stood up, "Good job, son!" and clapped Tommy on the shoulder. "Now on this back one I want you to stay as close to the bed as you can. I want to use these back two fenders on the trailer we are going to build. That's when I'll start teaching you to weld. In the meantime, let's get these fenders off." Tommy's dad grabbed a handful of longnecks out of the refrigerator and kicked back to watch his son work. With each fender the lines were straighter and the cuts cleaner. As each fender fell Tommy's dad let out a cheer. When the truck was free of its fenders, Tommy's dad put away the torch and handed Tommy the keys.

"Park this out by the tractors. It's your practice vehicle so you can learn to drive, also so you can learn metalworking. Next weekend you can cut off the doors."

FARM WORK

They're out there again today, from dawn until dusk, like always. The two ancient men, crusty, dried and brittle, they are beyond the age that their number of years on earth can be guessed from observation. Placed strategically in their webbed aluminum lawn chairs, they appear as gargoyles guarding the tarnished Airstream trailer from the onslaught of the natural world. Their efforts fail as vines and bushes obliterate all but the entrance and the hard packed patch of dirt where they keep vigil. A wilted pecan tree shades the gerontic stewards from the blazing Texas sun. Later in the year, when an occasional coastal wind finds its way across the savannah, the tree may be coerced into giving up a generous load of tiny native pecans. Today, its only purpose is shade.

"Well, boy, about time to cut the hay," states the smaller man, gazing across the field from under the edge of his sweat-stained fedora.

"Reckon so," the larger man replies. He slowly stands, putting his hands on his knees for support. He walks beyond the perimeter of the shade and places a gnarled hand to his forehead. The sunlight glistens on the mist of perspiration accenting the maroon and purple lesions on his bald pate as he surveys the uniformly tall stand of reedy grass covering the 40 acre field.

"Good crop this year. Might get three cuttings," he states.

"If it rains," says the father.

The son returns to his chair and settles back in, adjusting his weathered body to a position of least discomfort. The father pulls a small, flat bottle from among the folds of his oversized denim coveralls. He unscrews the black plastic cap, takes a small sip and passes it to his son. The son reaches with both hands. The fingers of his right hand encircle the bottle while he supports the bottom with the back of his left hand. The strange disease that turns his body to stone has made it difficult to grip with any force. After repositioning his hands, he's able to get the bottle to his mouth for a drink. He passes the container of warm brown whisky back to his father who closes it and puts it away. Time passes quietly and with little discernible motion under the pecan tree. An old spaniel looking dog of questionable ancestry twitches in his sleep while lying in a depression at the base of the tree. Its only functions are keeping renegade skunks out from under the trailer, disposing of the meager remains of the old men's dinner and providing comfortable accommodations to a large population of fleas. The dog raises his head and looks toward the meandering two lane blacktop road that passes by across the drainage ditch. Soon the neighbor boy rides his bicycle into view. He rides slowly, aimlessly, his eyes focused on the clover filled ditches that line the narrow lane.

*****

Tommy finished his morning chores hours before and had a while until he needed to exercise the horses. His little brother and sister were building a hay fort from the bales of redtop cane in the barn. Tommy was too old for that nonsense. Besides, the hay made him itch. He decided to take a bike ride. His bike always seemed to have the same destination lately, down the road past Mr. Eli's place and right on the dirt road that was a shortcut over to the highway. On that road was a small lot of less than an acre. The widow Agnes Parsons had cut the lot from the back of her spread after her husband passed many years ago. She'd sold it to a man from town. Tommy didn't think anything of it until one day last fall when he happened by the lot and saw a family working to clear the brush, a dad, a mom and a young girl. He did a double take when he realized the girl was Tina from his class at school. She wasn't wearing the frilly dresses and patent leather shoes she wore at school. She had on jeans , boots and a long sleeved denim shirt. Her wavy cotton-blond hair was tied up in a red bandana. She was mowing the grass - on a tractor! So now anytime he takes his bicycle out for a ride it seems to guide him toward this lot. Today he was still on the paved road when he heard a man's voice.

"Hey, boy, c'mere!" It was old Mr. Eli calling him. The father stood up from his chair, stretching, letting the rigor slip from his muscles. By the time he'd walked to the edge of the shade, Tommy had wheeled his bicycle up the driveway and slammed on his coaster brake. Loose gravel skittered across the dust.

"Good morning Mr. Eli." Tommy said, leaning his bike against the old man's truck and removing his baseball cap.

"Mornin', boy. Tommy ain't it?" The withered man asked.

"Yes, sir."

"Your dad has the stables that butt up to the back half of my field, right?"

"Yes sir."

"Could you ask your dad to stop by? I'd like to ask him if he'd be willing to bale my hay. Y'all have the equipment, don't you?"

"Yes sir. we have a windrow rake, a baler and a brand new sickle mower so the grass don't get beat up so bad like with a shredder. Problem is, Dad's got a full-time job now. He's working for Daddy Dow. He works six nights a week in the mag-cells - graveyard shift. He's not takin' on no outside farm work but maybe I can do it for you."

The old man looked a little surprised. "What are you, about nine?"

"I'm eleven, sir, be twelve next month. I baled our back pasture." Tommy lied, but only a little. He had cut and raked the field with the little Farmall 'C' but his dad had driven the big Case that pulled the baler.

"Well, I don't know. Ask your dad to call me. If he says it's okay with him, it's okay with me."

"Mr. Eli, that's Johnson grass, ain't it? My dad says you should just burn it off and plant some Coastal or alfalfa that's worth something."

"Well, boy, I appreciate the input but you can't kill off Johnson grass by burning. It grows underground like the Devil and, like the Devil, fire just makes it stronger." A slight grin cracked the old man's face.

"If you want it baled I can do it. I'll have him let you know in the next day or so."

"Be quick about it. It's starting to head out so it's not going to grow any taller. If you do a good job you can bale my next cutting too. You don't have to worry about hauling it. I sell it in the field. Get me a price per bale."

"Yes sir!" Tommy jumped on his bike and headed for home. He had forgotten all about Tina. As he approached his house he began to have second thoughts. He knew he could cut and rake the field. It was a clean field, no trees or stumps. The only problem was the baling. The little Farmall wouldn't run the baler. The Case would but it didn't have electric start. He'd seen his dad with the crank shoved into the front of the tractor cranking and cussing and getting thrown in the dirt by the recoil. He knew there were tricks to starting it, priming the carburetor, adjusting the spark advance and even then sometimes the tired old machine refused to fire. He'd helped his dad pull start it with a tow chain in the Spring when it hadn't been started for a while. It took them half a day to get it going.

Tommy had a lot to think about as he exercised the horses through the afternoon. He had to approach his dad about his offer to Mr. Eli. He was worried about his ability to get the Case started. He didn't have any idea what to charge for the job. He wanted to make sure and schedule the job so he would be doing the baling on the weekend to be sure Tina saw him operating the huge Case tractor while baling 40 acres of hay. He decided he'd wave to her nonchalantly as he made one of the many passes through the field across the street from her family's lot.

Tommy brushed out the mane and tail of the last mare of the day and fed all the horses. He entered the house and washed up just as his mom was setting the table for dinner. His dad was sitting at the head of the table, his usual spot, staring into a cup of black coffee. Tommy missed spending time with his dad but knew his dad felt good about elevating the family's standard of living. Tommy took his regular seat at his dad's right hand. His brother and sister were creating a screaming ruckus in the adjoining living room.

"Dad, I got a job offer," Tommy said. Dad's gaze shifted from his coffee to Tommy's eyes and stuck. Mom suddenly found a seat at the table. Even the noise in the next room diminished as if Tommy had crepitated in living color. "Mr. Eli wants me to bale his hay. Actually, he wanted you to do it but I told him you were too busy," Tommy stated.

"Oh no, no, nope! Not a chance!" his mom interjected. That's when Tommy knew he had a chance.

"Wait just a minute. Let the boy talk," Dad demanded.

"You know I can do it," Tommy spoke directly to his dad as mom glared and fidgeted. "The only thing I might need help with is getting the Case started and setting up the twine feed on the baler. You can go over that with me on your day off."

"This is a bad idea!" Tommy's mom hissed and stomped back toward the counter.

Dad just shook his head. "When does he want it done?"

Tommy saw a ray of hope. "The grass is headed out. I thought I could cut on Thursday, rake on Saturday and bale on Sunday."

Tommy's dad glanced toward the kitchen where Mom was violently shredding lettuce with her bare hands. "That might work. I'm off Sunday night so if I have to stay up to help you get the Case going I can sleep later. Once it's warmed up it's easy to start." By this time Tommy's little brother and sister were standing by the table awestruck. Tommy's chest was about to explode.

"Can you let Mr. Eli know it's okay with you?"

"I'll stop by and talk to him on the way home from work in the morning. You make sure and do a good job and you could get more work out of it."

"Dad, I don't know how much to charge. He wants a price per bale." Tommy waited while his dad rubbed the stubble on his chin.

"I tell you what," his dad offered. "Why don't you take all the costs into consideration and come up with a number? Tell me what you come up with and I'll see if you're in the ballpark."

Tommy wolfed down his dinner while his mother continued to fume. He even let his little brother have the last pork chop without confrontation. He immediately excused himself to his room, eager to do math. The irony of this was lost on him in the excitement. He knew some of the costs such as gas and twine. He guessed at how many bales the 40 acres would produce. He'd worked hauling hay the last couple of summers so he knew the thick stand would produce at least 600 bales. Most prairie hay brought in just under two dollars a bale in the field at 1968 prices. He would need at least 30 gallons of gas and six rolls of twine.

Tommy's dad was pulling on his steel-toed work boots. Tommy's mom had her arm slung across his shoulder. She smiled at Tommy as he came into the living room with his notebook paper covered in figures. It was encouraging to see that the tension had dissipated.

"Let's see what you came up with," Tommy's dad said, reaching for the paper. He studied it for a few minutes. "Your costs look accurate, or close. I think you will get closer to 800 bales but it's better to figure on the short side. So, you really like Mr. Eli?"

"Well, I guess - he's okay. Why?"

"Well, son, according to this, you're working for free. You didn't figure in any labor."

Tommy suddenly felt lost. Of course he wanted to make money, but how much? It would take three days of labor, or more like two half days and one full day. He grabbed the paper from his dad and ran back to his room. He knew if he turned around he'd see his dad and mom shaking their heads in amusement. Tommy finally figured that he'd like to make 150 dollars. He felt greedy. That was a huge sum for a twelve year old boy to make. On the other hand if he were an adult it would be meager pay. He could do just as good a job as an adult, couldn't he? By the time he finished his calculations his dad was walking out the door. He handed the revision to his dad.

"I'll look at this. We can go over it in the morning," his dad said, neatly folding the paper and putting it in his shirt pocket. Tommy stood silently by the door as his mom walked his dad to the truck and kissed him goodbye.

When his mom entered the front door she looked at Tommy. Her wet eyes sparkled as she pulled him into a hug. "You're growing up too fast," she said, her voice cracking. She released him and headed toward the kitchen.

The next morning Tommy went through his routine automatically. His dad had stopped on his way home and informed Mr. Eli that is was okay for Tommy to bale his hay but other than that it was between Mr. Eli and Tommy. When he got home Tommy waited with chores completed.

"I looked over your figures. They look okay, pretty generous really. I stopped by and let Mr. Eli know that you have my blessing."

"Was he satisfied with the price?"

"We didn't discuss that. It's between you and him. I've got to get to bed. I'm pulling a twelve hour shift tonight."

Mr. Eli's son is named Bart. Everyone calls him that, the mailman, the barber, the widow Mrs. Parsons. According to Mr. Eli, even dogs call him Bart. When Tommy rode his bicycle into the driveway, Bart waved him over. Mr. Eli nodded in the lawn chair, snoring grandly, a stream of spittle running down his drooping jaw. Bart motioned for Tommy to wait so Tommy took a seat on the rusted chrome bumper of Mr. Eli's truck.

"Your dad stopped by this morning." Bart said. "He seemed confident in your ability to handle the job. You just have to get it passed my dad. He's skeptical."

Tommy looked over at Mr. Eli and shrugged. "I can cut on Thursday, weather permitting. The dew should be dry by ten, I figure."

"Poppa!" Bart shouted. Mr. Eli started awake, wiping his mouth on his sleeve. "Tommy's here." Mr. Eli shifted the fedora back on his head and stared at Tommy through ice blue eyes as his brain caught up with his consciousness. He fished the flat bottle from his coveralls and took a sip then held the bottle out toward Tommy.

"No thanks, Mr. Eli. It's a little early for me."

Bart snickered under his breath and reached for the bottle. Mr. Eli snatched the bottle back and snorted. He replaced the cap and shoved it down into the folds of his garment.

"So,---- your old man seems to think that you're capable of handling my harvest."

"Yes sir."

"Well I don't know. You look a little wet behind the ears to me."

"I'll tell you what, sir. Give me the chance. I'll cut and bale your hay for thirty five cents a bale on the ground. That's a good price. If it don't suit you, you don't pay. Fair enough?"

"Fair enough." The old man stuck out his grizzled hand and Tommy shook it firmly.

"I'll cut it Thursday. We'll take a look at it on Saturday morning. If it's cured I'll bale it Sunday as soon as the dew dries."

"That's workable." Mr. Eli said.

Tommy straddled his bike and rode away but he didn't go straight home. He rode back toward his house but instead of turning down the driveway he continued on down the road past the pecan farm to where the trees grew close to the road allowing the branches to intertwine above. Between the Spanish moss and the wild grape vines the sun was almost totally blocked, as if dusk had come at midday. Only small dappled patches of sunlight filtered through the canopy. The road descended into a low area through a swampy marsh surrounding a natural pond. A baby alligator ambled across the lane, picking up its pace slightly upon seeing the approaching bicycle. Tommy felt this place was his own, his secret, where he was at peace.

Wednesday Tommy spent his free time attaching the sickle mower to the Farmall. He checked the oil, aired up the tires and topped off the fuel tank in anticipation of the next morning.

The humidity was low for south Texas. Though school was out, it was still officially Spring, but the brutal coastal heat was radiant in the still air. The rains had slowed so much that cracks were beginning to form in the heavy clay soil. He planned for an early start upon awakening, if he could even sleep.

"Tomorrow's the big day," his dad mentioned that night at dinner. "Don't forget, you have chores here before you leave. if your job runs late maybe your mom and brother can exercise the horses in the afternoon."

"I guess we could cover that," Mom grinned, "but don't make a habit of it."

"Thanks Mom. I won't."

"We're really proud of you, son." Dad smiled and handed Tommy the last chicken leg, prompting an evil eye from his little brother.

Thursday started out smoothly. Tommy drove the tractor into the field just as the two old men stationed themselves beneath the pecan tree. He waved at them. Bart waved back and Mr. Eli touched the brim of his fedora. Tommy lowered the mower to cutting height, pulled down the bill of his baseball cap and engaged the blade. The crop was so thick he could only manage second gear. He began at the perimeter and worked inward. When he stopped for lunch around one o'clock he was disheartened to see how much of the field was left to cut. The afternoon went quicker as each pass grew shorter with the shrinking of the stand. By six p.m. he was done, dirty and exhausted. He was convinced he'd made a horrible mistake taking on such a job. When he returned home there were two places set at the table. Tommy washed up and joined his dad for a late dinner.

"Tired?" His dad asked.

"Sore!" Tommy replied.

"Just wait 'til tomorrow."

"I'll be fine"

His dad just smiled and attacked another spare rib. As it turned out his dad was right. When Tommy tried to roll out of bed in the morning every muscle burned. His dad was just getting in from work and he gave Tommy a pat on the back. Tommy tried not to flinch, but failed.

"Keep moving," his dad said. "You'll work that soreness out in no time."

Turns out his dad was right again. By the time he finished his morning chores he was moving at a more or less normal pace. No free time today, though. Tommy spent late morning switching out the implements on the Farmall and cleaning and servicing the equipment. Everything was go for Saturday until early afternoon when a couple of thunderheads built up to the southeast. Tommy watched them with an unfamiliar trepidation. Usually he could care less about the weather but a storm could delay the job or ruin the crop completely. He stood outside watching the sky and paced. The sky grew dark and the wind picked up sending powerful gusts through the brittle limbs of the oak in the back yard. After only a light smattering of huge raindrops the storm dissipated. Tommy had rarely experienced such relief. He still needed to exercise the horses before dinner.

Saturday morning Tommy slept in until 7AM. There was no hurry. The dew and residual rain had to be completely gone when he started raking. After his morning chores he fired up the Farmall and drove over to Mr. Eli's field. As he arrived, both of the old men were standing in the pasture kicking at the hay.

"Good afternoon," Mr. Eli said. "Sleep in?"

"Yep. No hurry, what with the rain last night."

"What rain?" Mr. Eli grinned. "I've made the ground wetter than that blowin' my nose."

"Does it look ready to rake?" Tommy asked, changing the subject.

"Looks okay to me. What do you think?"

"It's your hay."

"Rake it!" The old men headed back to their post by the trailer. The raking went much faster than the cutting. Tommy kicked the tractor into third gear and notched the throttle to full. Four hours later he was waving goodbye to Mr. Eli.

If ever a boy needed his father it was now. Tommy was out of his element. He'd driven the Case while pulling the twenty one foot disc.

He had no experience with the baler, a complicated contraption prone to malfunction. At dinner, Tommy had no appetite. He was pale and scared.

"How was your day? Did the raking go okay?" His dad asked.

"Really quick. Windrows are straight....but Dad? I've never run the baler."

"I guess you won't be able to say that after tomorrow.

"Yeah, I guess not." Tommy chose to let it pass.

*****

In the silent edge of dawn when even the roosters question the day, Tommy stands face to face with the massive Case tractor. The cold steel crank pulls his right hand toward the black earth causing his shoulder to slump. He shoves the heavy crank , the key to life for the colossal machine, into the dark orifice below the grill. He opens the fuel cock, sets the choke and the spark advance as he's seen his dad do. He checks the transmission. It's in neutral. Back at the front of the iron behemoth, he engages the crank and slowly turns the engine to the top of a compression stroke. Every muscle in his body tenses as he throws all of his energy into the revolution of the crankshaft. Nothing. The crickets chirp. The cicadas tease the sunrise. Tommy takes a walk around the tractor, checks the ignition switch and turns it on. He returns to the crank. Once again his muscles tense. Once again the engine spins. An explosive report awakens the morning, throwing Tommy's limp body into the dust. The world is awake yet the tractor is silent. A pair of headlights illuminate the driveway. His dad is home. Quickly Tommy slides the crank into its orifice. Using the sum of his will he thrusts every morsel of energy into the crank. The Case pops loudly falters and then catches, idling through the open exhaust. Tommy climbs up into the seat of the tractor. Ancient levers control the antique beast.

Tommy feels small atop the throbbing machine. A simple hook and eye hitch and spring locking driveshaft connect the baler to the tractor. The twine is threaded in the apparatus. Full rolls are in position for service. Tommy sees the decal, faded but legible, explaining how to thread the twine through the machine. He loads a half dozen extra rolls of twine into the cargo box and pulls the equipment out onto the driveway. He leaves the tractor idling and joins his father who's been observing from the fender of the truck. He notices the light flicker on in the kitchen window. The horizon begins its amber show.

"Looks like you have it under control," Tommy's dad remarks. Two proud men survey the scene.

"No dew this morning," Tommy says. "I can get an early start."

"Let's grab a bite first." The father and son enter the kitchen to the smell of coffee and bacon. After breakfast, Tommy rushes through his chores to the sound of the tractor calling.

Before Bart and Mr. Eli exit the trailer Tommy has lined the baler up with the outermost windrow. Tommy climbs down from the tractor seat as Mr. Eli carefully steps down from the Airstream.

"I didn't expect you this early," Mr. Eli says.

"The ground is dry. I thought I'd get an early start in case I run into some snags."

Old Mr. Eli seems to smile his approval but who can tell on a crusty face like his. Tommy mounts his perch atop the tractor and engages the PTO. The baler awakens, a monstrous iron lung breathing in grass and coughing out bales with a rhythmic mechanical pulse. Slowly the tandem mechanism lurches down the windrows spitting tight bales in its wake. As Tommy completes his second round he sees Mr. Eli dragging a sledge hammer and a yard sign to the corner of his property. The sign says simply "Hay for Sale".

It's about ten a.m. Tommy stops for a drink of water and to load the next rolls of twine. The bale counter is at 184. Four pickups, two with trailers, are parked at the entrance to the field. Tommy waves to several of his friends who are loading and hauling the hay. A couple of times during the morning, trucks follow the baler, loading the bales as soon as they are ejected. Every time Tommy passes the north side of the property, he checks the lot Tina's family owns. As of eleven-thirty there's still no activity. No problem. Tommy estimates that he'll bale over 800 bales for Mr. Eli. He's already planning what to do with his new wealth.

After several hours of baling the sun is directly overhead in the cloudless sky. The shadows have disappeared. The rhythmic churning of the machine becomes hypnotic. Tommy inches the tractor down the backbone of the endless hay snake while his mind wanders aimlessly to fishing the river with his little brother, spending some of his new wealth at the local skating rink and, of course, to Tina. There's still no sign of her family at the lot across the road. Suddenly a blaring truck horn brings him back to reality. Looking behind, he sees over a half dozen broken bales strung out behind the baler. He stops the tractor and disengages the PTO. The pulsing of the baler slows until only the low rumble of the tractor breaks the silence. The pickup that had been following backs away and heads for the entrance. Tommy opens the access panel and finds a tangled wad of twine the size of a basketball. Pulling out his pocket knife, he begins cutting and ripping at the mess until he's down to nothing but metal. He rethreads the twine according to the decal and latches the cover. He climbs back on the tractor and engages the baler. It sounds normal so he begins to slowly move along the windrow. He watches behind as the first few bales exit the chute. They're tied up but look somehow crooked. When he checks them he finds that one of the strings is tighter than the other giving the bales an unnatural curve. Tommy shuts down the machine and pops the access panel open again. Everything looks normal. He reads the decal and notices an illegible paragraph with arrows pointing to some adjusting rods. He checks them and observes that the lock nut has backed off on one. He adjusts the rod back to where the rust indicates a previous setting and tightens the lock nut. After latching the door he cuts the strings on the misshapen bales and resumes baling. All goes well. He turns the baler around and repairs the broken bales then continues down the windrow. Soon another crew is in the field loading the bales as soon as they leave the chute.

As Tommy loops around the north side of the field he sees Tina standing at the driveway to her family's lot watching as he comes closer. She waves. He waves back. The next time he comes around Tina is standing at the edge of the field holding a blue plastic tumbler. Tommy shuts down the baler and dismounts. Tina meets him halfway across the field.

"You look like you could use some tea," she says. Tina hadn't said that much to him the entire time he'd known her.

"Thanks," he replies. "It's pretty hot out here. I need to finish this today so I'm working through lunch. I sure do appreciate the tea."

"Sure. You live around here?"

"See that big silver barn behind the pasture?"

"Yeah."

"My house is behind it."

"We might be neighbors soon. My parents want to build out here."

"That'll be good. Not very many kids from our class live out this way. Jerry Sullivan and Arty live off the highway at the end of the road but that's a mile away."

"Yeah, I know them. Jerry's a little weird but Arty's okay."

"Jerry's alright too. He just likes everyone to think he's smarter than they are."

"That can get annoying."

"You just have to let it roll off of you."

"I guess."

"Well, hey, thanks for the tea. I better get back to work."

"Me, too. I'm helping Dad set some fence posts."

"That's hard work!"

"You're telling me! I'll see you. Holler if you want more tea. We have plenty."

"Thanks. See you later." Tommy floats back over to the tractor and begins making the slow circles again.

The western horizon is glowing a warm red when Tommy disengages the PTO and lets the baler slowly wind down. He pulls the contraption up to the front of the trailer where Mr. Eli and Bart lounge. Tommy looks at the field. Only a few dozen bales remain on the ground.

"What did we get?" Bart asked. Tommy checked the counter.

"Counter says 827 but I had to re-bale a few. Let's call it 800 even."

"You sure?"

"Works for me."

Mr. Eli pulls a wad of money from his coveralls and peels off 14 twenty dollar bills, handing them to Tommy. "Good job, son. We'll see you back in August if we get some decent rain in the meantime."

"Yes sir. Thank you."

"Hey Tommy," Bart hollers after him, "I think the little neighbor girl is sweet on you!"

Tommy just smiles and shakes his head hoping the darkness is masking the flush forming in his cheeks. He drives the tractor home and pulls it into the pasture. When he turns off the key the silence engulfs him bringing with it a level of exhaustion he has never experienced.

"Hungry?" Tommy's mom asks when she hears the screen door slam.

"Just a sandwich, I'm too tired to eat."

Tommy's dad is kicked back in his recliner reading a *Horse and Rider* magazine. "How'd you do?"

"Made 800 bales. What do I owe you? I used 6 rolls of twine plus what was in there and I'm pretty sure both tractors are almost out of gas."

"How about you cut and bale that ten acres in the back end of the pasture next month and we'll call it even."

Tommy grinned. "Sure, but I'll need some help putting it in the barn."

"That's what little brothers and sisters are for," his dad chuckled. His little brother looks up from the coffee table where he is building a model car and gives him the evil eye.

THE BRIDGE

Point your toes when you hit the water or your feet will split open, peeling the flesh up around your ankles. If you don't bend at the waist once you go under you'll sink to your knees in the mud on the bottom and drown before you can free yourself. The distance from the apex of the bridge to the water's surface is 66.6 feet. All sorts of rumors and horror stories surrounded the San Bernard River bridge. Some were loosely based on fact. Tommy suspected most of them were old wives' tales, the nightmare spawned fodder that made jumping from the high concrete bridge a death defying act of bravado for teenage boys. Supposedly, a boy from Sweeney jumped from the bridge a few years ago and hit a submerged log, splitting his body in two. Preston Clifton was the only boy who'd dived head first from the bridge and lived to tell about it. His dad was the preacher at the Church of Christ. He believed in predestination. He neither confirmed nor denied the act. When asked, he simply said, "I know the river I was baptized in wouldn't take my life." Supposedly, Ronnie Goalsby counted out loud to 14 from the time he jumped until he hit the water. Tommy doubted Ronnie could count to 14 under stress. He was as dumb as a mud fence. What he lacked in brains he made up for in size and meanness. Tommy hated him, and maybe feared him a little too.

Highway 288 crossed the San Bernard river bridge on the way to Four Forks, a four way stop with three churches and two liquor stores. Tommy accompanied his dad there on a regular basis, not for church. The little stop was just across the county line. Tommy's family lived in Brazoria county. Like many counties in Texas, Brazoria county was dry. You could buy beer in the county but if you wanted wine or liquor you had to go elsewhere.

The area under the San Bernard river bridge was beautiful, a lush flat grassland with abundant wildflowers. Wild onions grew in thick patches. The space of several acres was well maintained by the county. When they mowed, the aroma of onions filled the air with a promise of summer. It was only a few miles from home and Tommy frequently rode there on horseback with his family. They would pack a picnic lunch and swim in the river while the horses grazed on the lush vegetation. They never jumped off the bridge.

Once, before Tommy was a teenager, some boys he didn't know were jumping from the bridge. Tommy's mom was horrified.

"Don't ever even think of doing something that stupid!" She scolded. She had no need to worry. Tommy was terrified of heights. It had taken him a full six hours to work up the courage to climb the 10 foot ladder into the tree house they discovered in the back of their pasture even after his little brother and sister had shimmied up the ladder and taunted him.

It was a steaming hot July day when Tommy was out riding bikes with Jack and Mack Henson. They were twins but didn't look anything alike. Mack was thin and pale with an abundance of freckles. Jack was muscular and bronze with a measured way of moving. Mack was loud and challengingly rowdy. Jack had a dark, disturbed quietness about him that would push him to take his own life several years later. Today they brought their little sister, Rochelle. She had stringy black hair and green eyes. Her puffy pale skin seemed to always be fighting a mild case of acne. At fourteen, she was couple of years younger than her brothers and a year behind Tommy. Normally she would have been hanging out with Tommy's sister, Marcy but Marcy had gone to Houston with her Aunt Lois to shop for school clothes. Rochelle's thick legs were having trouble keeping pace with the boys and she'd started whining about it, threatening to tell her daddy that her brothers abandoned her. The boys were forced to wait so Mack and Jack could avoid a severe beating. Eventually the group found themselves at the San Bernard river about 4 miles from home. They were soaked in sweat. Since it was broad daylight skinny dipping was out of the question. The boys shucked t-shirts and jumped in with their shorts. Rochelle was wearing one of those frilly blouses that made her look even puffier than she was. She finally lost the blouse and jumped in with her shorts and bra. Tommy couldn't help but notice that the bra was too small. Rochelle's pale freckled skin was squeezing out in all directions from the dinghy white harness. He tried to look away when she caught him staring but all he could do was scrunch up his nose.

"That looks uncomfortable," he said.

"It is. I bet you'd like me to take it off," she said.

"I really don't care." He thought of Rochelle mainly as an annoyance that he had to tolerate because she was friends with his sister. Still, his body was responding to the conversation in a way that made his shorts feel too small. He was glad he was shoulder deep in murky river water.

"Let's jump off the bridge," Jack said.

"Dad will kill us if he finds out," Mack cautioned.

"Not if the bridge beats him to it." Jack was out of the water, sprinting up the embankment.

"Okay, I'm in," Mack said. "Tommy, you coming?"

"I don't think so."

"He's a pussy," Rochelle giggled and released her bra from underwater, tossing it into the grass.

"Are you chicken?" Mack asked. Jack was halfway up the bridge.

"I don't know. A chicken is a bird and a pussy is a mammal," Tommy said. He wasn't exactly blinding them with science.

"You should try it," Mack hollered back. "It's fun, better than a roller coaster."

"You don't even know what a pussy is," Rochelle whispered from just behind Tommy's ear. Two soft pencil erasers grazed his back. He stiffened, trying not to flinch and searched for words. No sound came out. Rochelle swam away.

Jack reached the top of the bridge. Instead of climbing over the rail and standing on the concrete ledge, he stood atop the metal rail. He wasn't looking down at the water. He peered straight ahead to the horizon, his future. Without warning he sprang high and away from the bridge. As he descended he stretched his arms wide and tilted his head back slightly, like a crucifix. Just before impact he brought his arms up and slipped into the water making barely a ripple.

"Show off!" Rochelle screamed. "I bet you can do better than that," she told Tommy. He felt the nipples again. This time a hand was on his waist then slipping down the front of his abdomen. She touched him there.

"Whoa! I guess you're not a queer after all," Rochelle whispered, "or maybe you just thought Jack's jump was beautiful."

Once again no words came to Tommy. Rochelle swam away. Jack surfaced.

"Oh my God!" Jack exclaimed. "Tommy, seriously, you have got to try that! It's like flying, maybe better!"

Mack was at the top of the bridge. He stepped over the rail and stood on the ledge. He looked at the water and quickly sat down on the bridge rail. He looked at his brother who was observing him without expression. He stood, looked down again and jumped. Arms tight to his side, eyes closed, he looked like a stick falling through the air. He tilted slightly backward before hitting the water and shot back out of the water feet first a few yards away. Jack swam out to meet him.

Tommy felt the breasts pressed firmly against his back. This time her hand found it's mark without delay. Her chubby little fingers gave a firm squeeze.

"Make the jump," she said. "I'll show you what I've got."

Tommy headed for the bridge. What exactly she meant by that he wasn't sure but he wanted to know the answer. As he climbed up, the bridge kept getting higher. The water was so far away. At the peak he stepped over the rail and sat. He looked down. Dizziness and nausea overcame him. No way he could do this. He was about to turn back.

"Jump! Jump! Jump!" Three voices in unison chanted loudly. He looked over and Rochelle was standing waist deep, her chubby little hands supporting her breasts as if offering a prize.

Tommy sprang forward flailing in the air. Halfway down he remembered, toes pointed, legs together. That was all he had time for before the impact stung the underside of his arms nearly ripping them from his torso. He was a spinning mass of arms and legs. His right foot and elbow touched mud. He panicked, began swimming toward the light. Was it the surface or The Light he had read about? Just before his lungs burst he reached air. His ringing ears heard a distant cheer.

He swam frantically to shore and lay gasping. His arms and shoulders were on fire. A grin came across his face as the endorphins negated the discomfort.

"Ready to go again?" Jack asked.

"Maybe later," Tommy replied.

By the time he regained his composure and got back in the water, Rochelle was securely harnessed in her bra. He spent the next half hour trying to decide how to approach her about claiming his prize.

Jack made three more identical jumps. No one else jumped again. Well before dusk they put their shirts back on and headed for home. They hadn't made it more than a mile when Rochelle started whining about being left behind. Tommy realized he didn't even want the prize.

VANISHING POINT

It's my day to scout the perimeter. Originally Bobo was the only resident allowed the privilege as he had been here for 16 years and developed a high level of trust with the administrators. He recommended me. We became friends almost instantly upon my arrival because we're both here by mistake. Unlike him, however, I have no plans to stay. It's only a matter of days before I'll be going home.

I don't have a background in security like I told the bosses. The closest thing to what I'm doing now is when I was a teenager I rode the fences on my paint mare to cool down after our training session. It was a good way to relax and unwind from the pressure of intense training. That's why I like this job. It gets me away from the main house and gives me time to meditate. I doubt I'll ever find a penetration in this fence. It is ten feet of mortared rock with another four feet of chain link topped by a dense coil of razor wire. It'd be unlikely that anyone could enter unscathed. Besides, it's not like there's anything of intrinsic value here, just some drugs and a few expensive, though highly specialized, machines.

I grew up in northwest Arkansas so I've seen beauty. The Ozarks have a natural radiance for every season. This place, however, with its manicured lawn and endless garden, is like paradise. The fence is the downside. Although it keeps the riff raff out it also prevents us from leaving. "Who'd want to leave paradise?" You ask. Well, in my case, I miss my family. Bobo is my only friend here. Everyone seems a little weird, especially the staff. If it wasn't for Bobo I'd likely go nuts.

The way I ended up here is a bit like one of those twisted mystery stories on TV where I'm the unjustly accused. I was driving along and suddenly there was a huge explosion. I figure it was like one of those IEDs that killed my brother in Iraq during the First Gulf war. I was three years older than him. According to my dad I was a mama's boy. When he'd get a buzz on he'd mention my lack of interest in contact sports. He always chided me for not going out for football. "Come on, son, you're tall and fast. You could be a running back or a wide receiver. It could pay for college." It was the "contact" part of contact sports that I found uncomfortable. Not the pain of being hit, I have a pretty high pain threshold. I just didn't like other guys in my personal space. To appease him I played baseball. I could hit okay but my fielding was atrocious. I also went out for track. I was good at long distance because of my height and I could set my body in motion, crawl up in my head and pound out the miles indefinitely. I tried a semester of tennis but my coordination, or lack of it, caused me to stumble. My mom had a cure for that. She enrolled me in ballet. I enjoyed it because I was allowed to hold and touch those beautiful ballerinas. Aside from the erotic tension it brought to my adolescent experience it had no positive effect on my athletic abilities. The fact that I enjoyed the classes really upset my Dad.

Once when he was toasted he even asked me when I planned to come out of the closet. Unfamiliar with the terminology, I assumed he had found my journal full of little stories I'd hidden there. Needless to say, I was at a loss for words. That disturbed him even more. Don't get me wrong I loved my dad. If I had been gay he probably would've found a way to deal with it.

So anyway, I didn't want my little brother to have to deal with this so I picked on him - for his own good. I'd pick fights or come up behind him and thump his ear, just generally harass him until he busted loose in a blind rage. Then I'd pin him until it passed.

"I'm just trying to make him tough," I told my Mom, "so Dad will like him." It worked too. He was the starting center on the high school football team from his sophomore year. He was picked as catcher on the all-state baseball team. The day he came back from meeting with the Army recruiter I pulled Mom and Dad aside. "See, it worked. He's a tough little shit. You can thank me for that." When he received his orders for boot camp he invited me to celebrate. We went on a camping trip to Lake Catherine. We picked up a pint of Jim Beam and hiked up the trail to the waterfall. Just as the full moon was rising we finished the bourbon. "I owe you," he said and proceeded to kick the crap out of me. "Now we're even." He gave me a hand up and helped me to the pool underneath the falls. "Clean up!" He tossed me in the water. We grilled a rack of ribs over the campfire while I dried out. The ribs came out perfect. The moonlight sparkled on the water while we discussed cars and girls and the future. That was the last time we did anything together, just the two of us. Less than a year later I waited with my parents on the tarmac as his flag-draped coffin was unloaded from a military transport.

I was married to Angeline by then and she was already showing. In fact, if you paid close attention at the wedding you could tell that parenthood was just around the corner. Angeline wasn't lean anymore. When I told her that her dark eyes got darker. ":Just messin'" I would say, "more of you to love." To be honest, I had never considered what it would be like to be a father. I was more than a little apprehensive. When little Rhianna was born it was like love at first sight.

I loved Rhianna and being a father. Angeline was a good mother, too, but it had been a rough and scary pregnancy and she didn't want to go through another one. We put all our energy into raising Rhianna. I don't know if it was our constant attention of if she was an exceptional child. She was a talented musician, an incredible athlete and by the time she was twelve she was reading four books a week between band and softball practice while maintaining an A/B average. When the pre-adolescent angst darkened the moods of her friends she remained positive, though a little confused. Fortunately, there was nothing going on in her life that she was not comfortable sharing with me or her mom. It was only a week before her thirteenth birthday. She asked to ride with me to the county line.

If it weren't for the Bible thumping bastards, we wouldn't even have been making the trip. The local churches had banded together to prevent the twentieth century from coming to our corner of mid-America one more time. I even showed up to testify at the public hearing. I was fighting an open container charge and I tried to explain to the commissioners that if they really didn't want people drinking and driving they should put liquor stores closer to people who drink. I even explained how it would keep the money in the local economy. It went before a public vote and the teetotalers managed to force their will on the general public once again. So we grabbed a cooler of ice and commenced our sixty mile round trip to the liquor store.

Rhianna was perplexed. She'd begun to notice boys and was trying to reconcile how cute they were with how goofy and stupid they acted. I gave her the standard line about how girls mature much faster, especially her.

"Okay, but how am I supposed to handle that? A lot of my friends act stupid around boys but that seems deceitful," she said. I told you she was smart.

"Hang out with the nerds," I joked. "They don't care what anybody thinks, plus they are the kids that will eventually rule the world!" I think that was the first time I consciously noticed that teenage eye rolling thing all parents complain about. I thought it was expressive and maybe a little endearing since she accompanied it with a grin.

"Dad, seriously, what do you think that would do to my street cred? "

"Your what? You mean farm road cred? Thicket cred? Hillbilly cred? Are you for reeeeal?" I had her laughing so hard she was gasping for breath.

"For reeeeal, dad!" She began after almost regaining her composure. "There is this one boy, he's more of a friend, really smart, draws crazy cool pictures. He thinks we should get together and put out a comic book. He actually calls it a graphic novel. I would write the story and he would make the art, like a collaboration."

"Yeah, sounds like fun," I said. "Something to do with all that spare time you have. I mean, who needs sleep, right? So, who is this wonder boy?"

"His name is Samuel. You know him."

"Little Sammy Harker?"

"He goes by Samuel, Daddy, and he's not really little anymore, just skinny."

"That's cool! It's fun to work with somebody on something you're both passionate about. So is he your boyfriend?"

"Not really, more like close friends. He's too shy for anything like kissing. He'd probably pee his pants"

Now it was my turn to bust a gut laughing. That little girl had it going on! We cut up and verbally sparred all the way to the county line. I thought how lucky I was to have Rhianna for a daughter. I didn't have anything to worry about. She would take the world by storm.

We purchased a case of beer and a quart of vodka. I picked out two 4-packs of those nasty little wine coolers for Angeline. That would be about a six month supply for her. We stashed it all in the back of the truck. Rhianna grabbed a big blue Gatorade and I picked up two 24 ounce Heinys for the trip home. Back in the truck Rhianna gave me that look when I popped open the Heiny, the one that reminds me how much she looks like her mother, the "I see you" look, like I'm about to be in deep shit. Then she just kicked off her shoes, put her feet up on the dash, angled her seat back a notch and took a deep chug on the Gatorade, leaving little blue traces down her dusty chin.

"At least she has my feet." I thought, as her long thin toes wiggled against the warm windshield. "Damn, it's hot!" I screamed when the little bare section of my back between my t-shirt and jeans seared against the vinyl seat. The AC had gone out about six months before but who needs AC in the winter? With late spring whispering hints of summer, AC repair was making its way up the priority list.

"We've got 2-70 AC today, girl. Let's crank the windows down and put the pedal to the metal." The first Heiny disappeared within minutes. I handed the second one to Rhianna. "Pop this open for me will ya' darlin'? I'm driving."

"Really, Dad?" She gave me that "Mom" look again so I rolled my eyes at her. I thought we were going to get in an eye rolling contest when she finally dug my church key out of the console and opened the beer.

"Toss this," I told her handing over the empty.

"Litter bug!" She barked.

"Open container law! Blame the idiots!" I barked back. She threw the green bottle into the grassy ditch. We settled in for the trip.

The wind in the cab made it difficult to converse. Rhianna stared out the open window at the green pastures and thick amber stands of winter wheat. Occasionally a vast field of red dirt stretched to the horizon with tiny green shafts of corn in perfect military formation. Rhianna put her hand out the window. Her long flexible fingers played in the wind like the flaps on an airplane wing. It was a dance or an air show. I couldn't take my eyes away. Then the explosion, the pain, disorientation. Was I upside down, airborne, in a barrel roll? An abrupt impact. Blackness.

In the thick gooey edges of some other universe, distorted sounds echoed through the sludge. Murmuring in some vaguely familiar language, machine sounds, a rhythmic piercing pulse combined in an aural soup. Is this Purgatory, the gates of Hell? Intense pain lent a smoky burgundy to the black fog. I was afraid to open my eyes but I had to know. Just the movement required to lift my eyelids sent screaming pain ripping through my head. Nothing looked familiar. I closed my eyes. Parallel green bars were etched on the back of my eyelids from the fluorescent assault. I lost my grip on conscientiousness.

Sometime later the sounds began to penetrate the mire. I lay still and listened. The murmurs became voices. I heard my name. Response was just too difficult. I lay still trying to make sense. The explosion, the world disintegrating, flying weightless then the final blast, I seemed to have survived - maybe. I couldn't be sure.

"Rhianna!" I must have screamed. The voices intensified, growing more animated. Flaming hot pain was ripping me apart. I was slipping away. *"No!"* I thought. *"I have to see Rhianna, to make sure she is alright."* I forced my eyes open ever so slightly. I saw two people I didn't recognize leaning over me. In the background was Angeline or someone that looks like her. "Angeline." I whispered, but she turned and sliped away. Maybe she wasn't there. Suddenly one of the people leaning over me shined a brilliant white beam in my eye, ripping a hole through my brain. I quickly closed my eye but the man forced it open flooding the interior of my skull with intense white pain. Once again the darkness saved me. That was nine days after the explosion. It took another three days before I could communicate. I wish that day had never come.

The dust in my mouth kept my tongue from moving but my ears were clear. I discerned that I had a broken leg, a broken back, several broken ribs, facial lacerations and a severe head injury complete with brain swelling requiring removal of a portion of my skull. According to the doctors my prognosis was good. *"What?! Are you listening to yourselves? That doesn't sound good!"* If I could only talk I would explain to them how ridiculous that sounds. I'd heard nothing about Rhianna. They were referring to the explosion as an "accident". *"Bullshit! Somebody blew us up! Either an IED or a grenade launcher. The damn terrorists were striking at the heartland of America!"* I grunted to get their attention. A nurse turned toward me.

"Rhianna?" I could only whisper.

"I'll be right back." The frightened nurse made a beeline for the door. My ability to judge time was still in a state of disarray but it seemed like hours before anyone came back into the room. Finally a young woman, a girl really, in a brightly flowered blouse came in shadowed by a disheveled and shrunken version of Angeline.

"How are you feeling Mr. Watts?" The girl asked.

"I hurt," I mumbled."Word is I'm going to survive. How's my daughter?" Angeline looked out the window. I could see the muscles in her face and jaw tighten.

"I'm sorry Mr. Watts, Rhianna didn't survive the accident." The girl looked genuinely sorry. I felt a blow to that thing people call a soul that resides in my chest. I thought I would implode. Angeline bit her lip and squeezed her eyes closed so tightly that tears literally squirted from the corners. I had to set the record straight.

"There was no accident. It was an explosion. We were attacked. Has anyone tried to find out who did it?"

Angeline whimpered a low moan. Her face was buried in her hands.

"Maybe I should let you have some time with your wife. I'll be right outside. If you need me just press your call button." The girl put a rubber cylinder in my hand. No sooner had the door clicked shut than Angeline pulled her chair only inches from my bed rail. There was a look on her face that I had never seen before.

"What the hell were you thinking?" She growled. "You killed our daughter! Are you crazy? You hit the damn bridge rail! You'd been drinking!" Her voice began to falter.

"We were attacked! I was there. The truck was blown off the road!"

She gave me a look like I was a figment of her imagination, like she didn't even believe I existed. "I read the police report. You lost control."

"The police? They weren't there. I was! If they're telling you that crap then they're covering something up!"

"Oh Jeff, damn it, you killed her. You should have been paying attention. How many times did I tell you not to drink and drive? Not only is our daughter dead but they are going to arrest you as soon as you heal up."

"I only had one beer and we were attacked. You need to help me find out who did this. It doesn't surprise me that the terrorists have hit rural America but it does surprise me that the local police would help cover it up. When is Rhianna's funeral?"

"It was last Saturday."

"What? You didn't even wait for me? What were you thinking?"

"They were only giving you about a 25 percent chance of regaining consciousness. At least you beat those odds." A brief relaxation of her facial muscles hinted at a smile. She took my hand. "What are we going to do?"

"We need to find out who did this and make them pay! I'll be up and around soon and we will sort this out."

Angeline rose from her chair and walked to the window. She opened the curtains as far as possible and stood staring out into the bright sky for quite some time. "I don't know," she said. "I've got to go." She left without looking at me again.

Later that evening a close cropped kid in a brown suit and patent leather shoes entered the room. "I'm Lawrence Burns. Your wife asked me to take a look at your case. Can we talk?" He stood just inside the door clutching a thin manila folder with both hands.

"I don't have a case. I was attacked, probably by terrorists. The bastards killed my daughter."

"Okay, well, according to the police report you hit a bridge railing, became airborne and landed upside down in a dry creek bed. They intend to arrest you for murder by auto. I think we can get it reduced to negligent homicide. What I would like to do for the time being is to use the statutes to force them to go ahead and serve the arrest warrant so the state will be responsible for some of the medical bills. Your wife tells me that money is getting tight." The kid wouldn't meet my gaze. He continued rifling through the three or four pages in his manila folder.

"Maybe you didn't hear me, you little shit!" The kid was obviously clueless. "We were attacked. Apparently, for some unknown reason, the police are covering it up. If you want to work for me you need to crawl out of the cops back pocket and find out who is responsible or when I get out of here I will and it won't be pretty! If you want to help me, fine. Otherwise, I need to find somebody with enough balls to stand up to the police. Go home and think about it. Get back to me."

"I'll see what we can do," he said, slinking out the door

Great, I've got an idiot for an attorney." It was definitely time for some pain meds.

I was just finishing my breakfast the next morning when Angeline arrived with Lawrence Burns by her side. She looked better than she did the last few times I'd seen her. She dressed conservatively elegant and had on her business face. Unfortunately, she was flanked by the sniveling Burns who looked terrified. Angeline took my hand.

"Sweetheart, you've met Mr. Burns. I've hired him to help us with our situation. He has a pretty good record on cases like ours."

"Terrorism? He has a background in bombings?" I asked.

"Yeah, all sorts of things like that." Angeline was selling the kid but I trusted her at least.

"Okay, what's the plan?"

Lawrence spoke up. "Mr. Watts, the police will be here in a few minutes with an arrest warrant. Try to be neutral and don't under any circumstances answer any questions or offer any comments. We'll save those for court. The less they have from us the better. Okay?"

"Okay." I didn't feel like talking to the cops anyway. Sure enough, not ten minutes later in walked two uniformed officers from the county. One was a young rookie. The other officer had given me the damned open container ticket.

"Good morning, sir. Are you Jeffery Watts?" The rookie asked.

"Yes"

"You are under arrest for the murder of Rhianna Watts by auto and for driving under the influence. You have the right to --

"I know my God damn rights!" I hissed.

"Fine, sir. We would like to ask you some questions."

"I don't intend to answer any questions on the advice of my attorney."

"Officers, if you don't mind, Mr. Watts has suffered severe head trauma and is on powerful medication. It would be in everyone's best interest to wait until he recovers. I'm sure he'll be willing to cooperate at a later time," Burns stated.

"You smooth talking son of a bitch." I thought. My respect for Lawrence Burns ratcheted up a notch.

"Fine," the rookie stated. "We're notifying the hospital director. As soon as he feels you're ready to be released we'll be taking you into custody. Be advised, you are under arrest and you are not to leave the hospital premises unless accompanied by an officer."

"I'm not going anywhere," I stated. The officers filed out. The older officer had yet to say a word. As soon as the officers exited, Angeline and Mr. Burns took a seat.

"The next step is to get the doctors to order a stay in a long term rehab facility, as opposed to jail time, while you await trial. It'll be their dime," Burns suggested.

"What about bail and just going home?" I asked. It seemed like the obvious answer to me.

"We'll see what the judge says," Lawrence said. "I'd imagine it is going to be prohibitively expensive. You're looking at two felony charges and to top it off it's an election year. The county attorney is up for reelection and he's not going to want to appear as though he isn't tough on crime."

"Sounds like my lucky day," I mused.

"Honey, with the funeral and medical expenses we're out of money. Your parents are covering Mr. Burns' fee but they're stretched pretty thin."

"Fine, but how am I going to locate these terrorist bastards from a 'facility'? It's obvious the cops either don't buy my story or they're part of the problem."

"Let's take it one step at a time. Okay, Honey?"

I could tell when Angeline was being condescending but I also knew she was right. We were broke.

There were no holes in the fence. I expected that. There *were* holes in the entire story from the police. I had no idea how deep it went at first, but after explaining to Bobo what happened he came up with a theory. The more I walked the perimeter and meditated the more sense it made. I was putting the pieces together. It wasn't just terrorists, at least not foreign terrorists. It was obvious if you thought about it. The next time Angeline came to visit me I asked her the question that confirmed my suspicion.

"Did you see Rhianna's body?"

Her color evaporated as her breathing became shallow. She looked right through me and became mute. "I have to know," I demanded. Tears began flowing. She got up to leave. I had to grab her firmly by the forearm to get her to stay. For a moment I saw fear in her eyes but she sat back down.

"Jeff, really. Do we have to go through this?"

"It's important."

"Damn Jeff! She was in several pieces. She went through the windshield. The truck rolled over her and she was caught up and flung through the brush. It was a closed casket funeral!"

"I knew it! It wasn't her. She's probably still alive somewhere."

"Oh, God, Jeff! Please stop it! They even did a DNA test. It was her! Can't you just face it? We need to move on."

"A DNA test, right? That's what Bobo figured they would use. Don't you see, Honey? She was so smart and capable. She's probably in a CIA training camp. If I can just get out of here I know I can find her!"

Angeline jerked her arm away. Her breathing was rapid. Tears streamed down her face. I think maybe I'd given her some hope.

I figured if I acted exactly like they wanted me to I could shorten my stay. I had to work out how to get to the source and find out the truth. I needed a clear head for that. I'd stop taking my meds. I figured if I didn't give anybody any shit I could probably hold them in my cheek and spit them out. Unfortunately, I wouldn't have Bobo's help anymore. He'd already told me that he couldn't hang out with me if I wasn't on my medicine. It was a trade off. Another trade off I soon found out was that when I didn't take my meds I thought about Rhianna all the time. That's not so bad, though, since I knew she was alive. Still I spent a lot of time alone now so no one would notice the change in my behavior.

Easter Sunday, I'd been here the better part of a year. The tedium of waiting for a trial was trying my patience. Church was coming to our little corner of Crazytown. I wanted to hang out with Bobo too. I missed him. He had to be here somewhere, probably in a garden. That's where we usually talk. My counselor asked me to go to church with him. He knew I'd been thinking of Rhianna a lot. He thought it might help me with "closure". The only closure I was looking for was a closure to my time here.

After flushing my morning meds, I greeted my counselor when he knocked on my door.

"What are you doing here on Sunday?" I asked.

"I figured I'd hang out here today. I really don't have a life outside of this place."

"Well I do," I said. "Why don't we trade places?"

He grinned. "Let's do church."

"I don't know. I've never been very religious."

"Me either, but I can often get some peace from a good sermon. It helps me get centered."

"What the hell. It's not like I have a lot on my plate today." I was actually hoping to run into Bobo so I could tell him what I'd discovered about Rhianna.

As we entered the meeting hall, which was really the rec room without the furniture, a grey haired woman was hunched over the piano hammering out high energy gospel strains. A mixed race choir of mostly middle aged women and very old men was beginning to assemble on a small set of portable risers next to the piano player. Two thin teen aged boys with spotlessly clean translucent skin were hefting a tall metal podium in through the back door. They set the gray metal stand in front of the choir, picked up a couple of small cardboard boxes and began handing out programs.

"Welcome. God Bless You. Praise Jesus! Peace Be With You!"

"Right." I looked around as the residents began filing in, No sign of Bobo. My counselor ushered me toward the front of the crowd and we sat in the first row of folding chairs. One of our maintenance workers rolled out a long strip of blue masking tape about eight feet in front of the podium. Two of our larger orderlies took position on each side of the rather surprised choir members.

"What is this, a church service or a rock concert?" I asked the counselor.

"We can't be too careful. As you know, some of these people are crazy," He stated. "I wouldn't cross that line if I were you."

I couldn't tell if that was a warning or a statement. I had no intention of finding out. As the last of the residents were seated the choir began with a slow acapella worship song, a standard that I vaguely remembered from my childhood when various friends would drag me to their church to make brownie points with their Sunday school teachers. I didn't mind. They usually fed me pretty well, either at a church potluck or going out after. My parents liked to sleep in on weekends. I later learned that was when they had their "romantic" times. It seemed like a win - win to me. The song also reminded me of Rhianna. Her voice would have improved the sound of the choir. The next song was a high energy praise song causing the choir members' blue robes to sway in unison like loblolly pines in a brisk March wind. Beads of perspiration were forming at the hairline of the piano player. The temperature of the room was rising. The song ended and the back door opened, silhouetting a tall, pencil thin man. As he approached the podium, piercing gray eyes surveyed the crowd. The nostrils of his hatchet shaped nose flared against the ashen paper thin wrinkles in his face. As he performed a loose jointed jog up the podium steps his oversized grey suit fluttered like a bird. Fluorescent lights sparked off his oily slicked back hair and mirror finish black shoes. Several heavy gold rings hung on his bony fingers as he raised his hands above his head.

"Praise the Lord! He is Risen! Rejoice, my brothers and sisters, rejoice!" He paused for effect.

"Amen!" shouted several members of the choir. The preacher had the same uncanny ability of an eighteenth century portrait to stare right through you. No matter where in the room you were, his red rimmed eyes looked into you.

"We are here today to celebrate! It is a day of joy, a day of forgiveness, a day of renewal! Praise Jesus!"

"Praise Jesus!" The choir answered.

"We're here today to talk about sacrifice. We're here to talk about undying faith. We're here today to talk about unconditional love! Can I get an Amen?!"

"Amen!" The choir answered along with several of the residents who were getting worked up.

"I'm here to share an amazing story. Do you know this story? It's the story of your salvation, a story of a one way ticket, a free ticket, A ticket that is redeemable - redeemable for your soul! A ticket to everlasting life! Everyone here can receive this ticket, right now - today! Amen"

"Amen!" repeated the robots. This was starting to sound like a midnight infomercial. I began to see a level of strangeness in this man that I hadn't previously noticed. His eyes started to glow. His flailing arms took on the inhuman flexibility of two snakes dancing around a flame.

"Let me share this story!"

"I know the story but I have a couple of questions," I blurted out. My counselor put his hand on my knee. I immediately pushed it away. The preacher took on the countenance of a pre- school teacher except his stone gray eyes retained their coldness.

"Of course, sir. I'll help you any way I can. That's why I'm here. What's your name?"

"I'm Jeff."

"Well, Brother Jeff, what are your questions?" He took a couple of steps toward me.

I stood up. "I'm not your brother. My brother died serving our country."

"I'm sorry to hear that."

"My first question is why you Christians, who are supposedly full ,of peace and love use a pre Christian torture device as your icon?"

"The cross represents the ultimate sacrifice Jesus made for the human race."

"We didn't ask for that! What kind of father would stand by and let his kid be tortured to death to prove a point? That's got to be one sick bastard! You worship him? What does that make you?" I was getting agitated but these are questions that bothered me for years.

"Can someone remove this blasphemer?" The preacher asked.

"So you can't answer that, you kid-killing son of a bitch!" I took a lunge at him to try to shut him up or shake some sense into him. "What kind of twisted fuck kills their own kid?" I was going for the throat. I would have had him, too, but one of the snakes must have bitten me and I had to take a nap. As the tiredness took over I saw Bobo behind one of the orderlies. He was shaking his head in pity. I just smiled. It was good to see him.

I slept through lunch and dinner and woke up hungry around midnight. Bobo reclined in the plush chair beside my bed. He was watching over me and a smile broke from his lips as he noticed my eyes open.

"Hey, Buddy, long time no see," I said.

"I've been around. You need to be careful who you piss off around here."

"Yeah, I screwed up. What happened after they took me out?"

"I don't know. I didn't stay either."

"Hey, I wanted to tell you, Rhianna's still alive."

"I wondered when you were going to figure that out."

"You knew?"

"Pretty sure. From what you've told me it just makes sense. Just because she's alive, however, doesn't mean she's safe. Some of the

CIA training techniques can be brutal especially in a situation like this where she's there against her will."

"I didn't consider that," I said, "but it does make sense. I've got to get out of here. Can you help me?"

"I don't know. Let me think about it."

Suddenly I heard a knock on the door. Bobo sprang for the bathroom. I pretended to be asleep. In a moment, the door opened. Housekeeping was doing a quick check on the room. She switched out the garbage bag, wiped down the end table and desk then headed for the bathroom. *"Oh shit!"* I thought. *"Bobo is going to get in trouble!"* I heard the toilet flush, the wastebasket being emptied and the shower curtain being pulled back. The maid came out of the bathroom and quietly left. Bobo never came out of the bathroom. I got up and went to tell him all was clear but he was gone. *"The man is a phantom."* I thought. *"If anyone can help me get out of here, it's him."* I sat up and read for a few hours hoping he would return but he didn't. I finally dozed back off.

When the nurse came to give me my morning meds, she asked for a pee test. "Just standard procedure," she stated. When she gave me my pills she waited while I took them, made me drink extra water and then rooted around in my mouth with a tongue depressor. I had no choice but to swallow the damn things. As soon as she left the room I went to the toilet and tried sticking my finger down my throat but, honestly, I've never been able to do that. I figured I would have another slow day walking the fence line. I ate breakfast just as the fog began to drift in. Around lunchtime, Lawrence Burns stopped by to see me.

"I hear you had a rough day yesterday." I could hear the sympathy in his voice. He was just a kid but I had him figured for a good kid with a good heart. I just wasn't real confident in his ability to go up against a government conspiracy.

"Yeah, I should never have gone to the church service. Me and God don't usually see eye to eye," I chuckled, trying to make light of the fiasco.

"I have a hearing scheduled for a week from tomorrow," he told me.

"Good! If we get a fair judge maybe I can get out of here and look for Rhianna's kidnappers. We can straighten this shit out."

"It's a competency hearing. I don't think it would be in your best interest to put you on the stand after what happened yesterday."

"Competency hearing? What the hell!" If anyone needed a competency hearing it was Burns. "Just let me explain the situation to the judge. I'm sure he would understand."

"I'm going to try to get the judge to keep you here. If you are judged to be competent you will go directly to jail and be tried for murder."

"Fine! Not a problem! I just need to get this over with."

"Jeff, there really isn't any evidence to support your version of the accident."

"Stop with the 'accident' shit! It was no accident. That's why I have to find Rhianna. When I prove she's alive the murder charge will revert back to whoever's responsible for her kidnapping."

"I think you should talk this over with your wife before you decide. I've asked her to stop by and see you this afternoon."

"Good. We'll get back to you. In the meantime, I know you're getting paid so you need to quit acting like a court appointed lawyer and move beyond this path of least resistance shit."

Burns exited. I began to wonder if maybe it wasn't time for a more aggressive attorney. This guy was a loser.

It would be wonderful to see Angeline again. I looked forward to the day our lives returned to normal and we could snuggle in bed on Sunday mornings with our coffee and honey buns, then afternoons watching Rhianna kick some ass on the softball field. While I waited for Angeline, I stopped by the rec room. There was Bobo watching a game of air hockey. He was hard to miss. At six foot four with thinning brown, shoulder length hair he resembled a lost grizzly bear. The years of incarceration had hunched his back but his face held a serene understanding.

"You up next?" I asked.

"No, just watching." He turned toward the garden. "We need to talk."

As we stepped into the garden, Spring overcame us. The sheer volume and intensity of the colors and scents temporarily sucked the thoughts from our minds and the breath from our lungs. Momentarily, the realization that I'd been there going on a year snapped me back to reality.

"I've got to get out of here!" I stated.

"As far as I can tell this facility would be almost impossible to escape from without outside assistance," Bobo explained. "Your best chances are to set up an escape while you're on the outside attending a hearing or jump through all the hoops and convince them that you're sane."

"They won't let me out of here. They know I know the truth and if I get out I'll dog their every move until I find Rhianna and then I'll bring them down!"

"Easy, Jeff." He could see I was becoming animated. "Let's not attract attention. I have some ideas. Do you think Angeline will help you from the outside?"

"Sure, she'd do anything I ask but I don't want to put her in jeopardy. What did you have in mind?"

"I'm working on it. If she can put some things in place on the outside maybe we can cover up her involvement."

I was warming up to his idea. "I'm going to see her this afternoon. I'll see if we can find a way to discuss it. What about locating Rhianna?"

"There really isn't much you can do from in here. I have some feelers out, contacts from my previous life."

"You had a previous life?"

"We all do. I'm safe here, that's why I'm not in a big hurry to leave."

"Well I'll be damned! You're a fucking spook! Whoda thunkit!

"Not really, but something like that."

As much as I questioned him he revealed little else. We ended up talking more about the plans I had when I was free to move about the community again. Even the chemical fog couldn't dampen my spirits now that the end was in sight.

So it was that I greeted Angeline with a beaming smile and open arms. Though her smile was tentative, her full body hug was reassuring. I guided her toward the garden where we could talk uninterrupted. Hopefully, we could have dinner together later, somewhat like old times.

"I miss you, baby," I said to her profile.

"I had to get a part-time job. I don't have much free time."

"Hey, as soon as I get out I'll make it up to you. You can take a couple of years off if you want."

"We'll see. We are up to our ass in debt and you might not even get out."

"Oh, I'll get out - one way or another," I said. She looked concerned.

"Jeff, please promise me that you won't do anything dangerous or stu--, risky, okay?"

"No, baby, it's nothing like that. It's just that I met a guy in here who has some contacts. I think he can help us." She looked at me like I was some foreign object that splattered down on top of her freshly baked reality.

"You've got to trust me. It's important." I took her left hand in mine and gently fingered her wedding ring. She reacted as if I had shoved an ice cube into her palm. I noticed an almost imperceptible tear form in the corner of her eye.

"We'll get her back," I said. "We can be a normal family again."

"Jeff, please! You've to get past this. She's not coming back. She can't. If you could just see it then maybe, just maybe, there would be hope for us. God knows I love you and I miss you so much. I know you're hurting. I'm hurting, too, but I don't understand what's going on. I don't even know who you are anymore."

"Well I'm not going to just roll over and let them steal Rhianna, that's for sure."

"Honey, I know it's hard for you but she's dead and there's not anything we can do about that."

"So you don't believe me?"

"I believe you miss her so much you can't let her go."

"There's more to it than that. Just wait. You'll see." I felt the discord leave her body through an audible sigh. Conflict resolved?

"This certainly is a beautiful garden." She focused on the landscape.

"Yeah, they spend a lot of time and effort making sure everything is just right. It'd be paradise if only you were here with me." She leaned over and kissed my cheek.

"Should we walk?" She asked.

"Sure, we have all the time in the world here. Will you stay for dinner?"

"I'll have to leave just after. I'm working nights at the Quickie Picky."

"I wish you wouldn't do that. You know night clerk at a C-store is one of the most dangerous jobs out there."

"It's what I can get and it keeps me out of our empty house at night, too quiet there."

When dinner time pulled us from the garden we found a table in the corner where we could sit together undisturbed. I saw Bobo observing us from across the dining area.

"It's almost like going out to eat," Angeline smiled, "at least for me anyway."

"My treat," I laughed. I was enjoying the light-hearted conversation but I had to broach one more subject. "Sweetheart," I began, "I may need you to help me with some outside contacts."

"Isn't that what Burns is for?"

"Call me nuts but I trust you a lot more than I do him. Besides, he really isn't putting forth much effort on my behalf. I promise I won't ask you to do anything illegal. It's just that I have to get out of here before I go crazy. The medicine they give me causes me to walk around in a stupor and I can't get anything done."

"You know I'll help wherever I can. I love you. I'm just not sure what to do."

"Me either, but I'll let you know as soon as I figure it out. Will you be at the hearing on Tuesday?"

"Of course, I'll be sitting right beside you. I already checked with Burns. He said it would be okay." She was smiling. It made parting easier.

As soon as she was gone Bobo was right in my face.

"Is she on board?" He asked.

"She said she would do what she could. Would you like to let me in on exactly what that is?"

"Let's see what happens Tuesday. We can figure it out from there. It may be a moot point."

The nurse from hell strictly enforced my morning medication. The evening staff was less persistent so I spent most of the week sleeping all day and reading and planning at night. I had to get some face time with the judge. For some reason Burns was against the idea. I wondered if he knew something I didn't. Was the judge involved? Could I trust Burns?

Tuesday morning came and, through no small effort on the part of Lawrence Burns, I was allowed to wear my own clothes to court in lieu of the orange jump suit provided by the county. Angeline was lovely in a crisp white blouse and knee length black skirt. Her curly black hair was pinned tightly back with the silver and turquoise barrettes I'd given her for our tenth wedding anniversary. Lawrence Burns wore the same cheap brown suit or an exact replica of it. I'd never seen him in anything else. The two cops from the hospital room sat next to the primped up blond woman I assumed to be the prosecuting attorney. For an instant I considered approaching her with my allegations then thought better of it. I'd promised Burns that I'd only speak if spoken to. I took Angeline's hand in mine, dwelling on the soft delicate fingers. I thought back to Rhianna's similarly slim fingers dancing in the air just before the explosion.

Enter the judge, an ample man with a trio of gelatinous chins stretching down from his thick jowled face. His black eyes form two limpid pools behind his wire framed glasses, giving him the appearance of a barn owl searching for prey. We all stand. The gavel falls.

The prosecutor is only a few lines into her opening remarks when I realize she may be on my side. She's convinced that I'm sane and should go to trial. I'm thinking that would be to my advantage. I turn to Burns and ask quietly if he's willing to work with her. He advises against it. I tell him It's my life and I should have some say. He shushes me and Angeline squeezes my hand, more firmly than I expect. The prosecutor wraps up her opening spiel. She hasn't mentioned anything about the explosion, only that I appear to be able to hold a conversation and I know right from wrong. I'm good with that.

It's our turn and Burns asks for a ten minute recess. The judge grants it. I'm guessing he already needs a cigarette break. As we turn to leave the courtroom I lose my balance and have to catch myself against the table. In the back row of benches sits Bobo with his fingers to his lips signaling me to silence. I acquiesce but it takes me a minute to regain my composure. He's dressed in street clothes. How the hell did he get here! As I walk out of the courtroom we exchange private smiles.

"This is a bad idea! You will go straight to jail!" Burns is flustered.

"Honey, aren't you more comfortable in the rehab center?" Angeline is anxious.

"Well let's talk about lowering bail. I mean, where the hell am I going to go?" She might be willing to do something there." I'm planning my moves. I pull Angeline and Burns into a quiet corner. "Did you see that big, brown-haired dude in the plaid shirt on the back row? He's helping me out. He's ex-CIA or some kind of spook but he knows shit. He knows Rhianna is alive and he's going to help me find her." Angeline and Burns look at each other, frustration obvious in their features. "Fucking ask him! He's right inside the door!" I can't believe they're not taking me seriously.

"We can talk to her about bail but I need you to admit that the possibility exists that you're wrong about Rhianna being alive," Burns insists.

"I'll say whatever I need to if I can go home," I tell him. "I don't have to believe it." Angeline glances toward the floor. "Look for the big lumber jack looking guy in the back row when you go back in," I say. "Don't acknowledge him, though, he wants to stay in the background."

We reenter the courtroom but Bobo has stepped out. Lawrence goes over to the prosecutor's table and sits down for a minute before they retire to the hall. The officers get up to join them but the prosecutor motions for them to stay put. It gives me an opportunity to stare them down, the bastards!

The state offers a two hundred thousand dollar bail. I can't afford to bond out so the trial resumes.

"All rise!" We go through that monkey business again. Burns gets up for his monologue. He rants on about head injury, post traumatic stress disorder and delusional behavior. The whole time I'm feeling it, the burning on the back of my neck. I know he's back. I don't want to cause a scene but I have to see. I sneak a glance behind me and gasp. The room goes silent. Angeline grabs my hand. "Eyes front!" She hisses.

There in the back row beside Bobo sits Rhianna. She sees me and smiles, giving me a little parade wave with her left hand. "Rhianna!" I scream. "I told you! See!" I jump the chair next to me and just clear the banister when the sergeant at arms tackles me and the two policemen pile on. I don't even care. I'm laughing. I know without looking that Bobo has escorted her out of the courtroom. I'm not worried. She is in good hands. It's all going to work out. Right now I just need a nap.

HEAT LIGHTNING

I must have been about ten. *It must have been Spring. The lemon tree outside my bedroom window was blooming so I had my window open just enough to smell the blossoms mixed with the rain. I don't remember why I was in bed but the storm precluded any outdoor activities. I was drifting in that peaceful place between sleep and consciousness when lightning struck the tree in the front yard. The explosion was deafening, causing me to jump up and strike my head on the bunk above me. A large limb sprang horizontally from the tree, landing 50 feet away. The voltage melted the telephone line that ran through the tree into a gooey smoke. I heard my mother scream in the kitchen and ran to find her twitching on the kitchen floor, the telephone receiver in her hand. I couldn't go to her. I couldn't touch her. I was afraid of the hoodoo, the black magic. Her eyes rolled back like those folks in the church my aunt dragged me to some Sundays. Would the spell creep up my arm? Would I be taken by the Spirit? My brother pushed past me and took her head between his hands, shaking her firmly.*

"Mama? Mama! Say something! Are you okay? She slowly quit trembling and regained a sort of connection with us.

"I'm alright," she said, but she wasn't, not really, not ever again.

The smell gave it away, especially walking here between the show barns and the midway. This was the last day of the county fair. The air felt sticky with the smell of grilling onions blown down the midway by slow rotating exhaust fans. Onions rarely finding their way to gastric indulgence, grilled simply to bring saliva to the mouths of prospective patrons, Pavlov's dogs. The odor of composting animal dung, pungent and earthy, combined with onions and people. Grandmothers smelled like pies and pickles. Young children, slamming wildly into each other like pool balls, yielded an odor of cotton candy. Teenage couples, attempting the physical impossibility of occupying the same space, mixed hormones and pheromones into a backseat cocktail of questionable decisions. Their bare arms and legs added this scent to the primal summer heat. Many of these folks were here to see me.

I heard the familiar slap of sandals running up behind me. I bent over slightly, bracing for impact. She was on me; arms around my neck, legs around my waist. Her dark curls mixed with my straight blond locks as she took my earlobe between her teeth. I made a playful attempt to dislodge her, whinnying like a bronco and spinning wildly. Just before slipping away, she stuck a moist tongue in my ear. Lily twisted free. I lunged for her, plucked her tiny body free of gravity and drew her toward me.

"Afternoon, sleeping beauty," I said. "You missed half the day."

"I've been up a while, took a shower." She pulled up the sleeve of her t-shirt and grabbed the back of my head, stuffing my nose into her armpit. "You should try it. We're hooked up to the water."

"I will," I said, "when I get ready for the show." I draped my arm over her shoulder but she wiggled free, pinching her nostrils between her fingers.

"And just end up sweaty again."

"So, it'll be clean sweat."

She rolled those dark eyes. "Mixed with gasoline and wood chips!"

"Then I'll take another one. You want some coffee or lunch?"

"I'm okay. Jerry bought me a burger."

"Jerry?" I asked. A hint of something I didn't want to acknowledge inflected in my voice. "What the hell did he want?"

"He wanted to talk to you about tonight's show."

"It's not a show, it's a competition. That sneaky bastard has something up his sleeve. I don't want you talking to him!"

"Excuse me!" The darkness in her eyes flashed metallic fire.

"I mean about the show, trade secrets and all that. You know." I thought I'd recovered, but some of the playfulness drained from the encounter. It's not that I didn't trust Lily but Jerry possessed that magnetic quality. I'd run in to him at a few events over the last couple of years. He usually had some starry-eyed fliptail hanging on him like a loose jacket. He's single now and all of a sudden he's our best friend.

"If you're hungry, I could fix you some lunch," she offered. "You have five or six hours before the show.

"Cool," I said. I was, in fact, hungry.

"Well c'mon then." She swatted my butt with her open palm hard enough to sting through my jeans. She ran. I caught her just as we reached the exit to the fairgrounds. I grabbed her hand, she leaned into me and we picked our way across the gravel parking lot to the exhibitor's section. I had one of the nicer units in the section. It wasn't the rolling palaces that the rodeo cowboys lived in but it beat the hell out of the camper shelled pickups that the flint knappers and gypsy traders inhabited.

I hooked up with Lily last spring. Since she began travelling with me she insists we roll out the awning, spread a rug under it and set out some patio furniture wherever we stop, even for one day. She's even picked up a couple of ficus trees in five gallon glazed pots that we drag out on the "porch" every time we set up.

Tonight's performance is the last of the season. It's the largest and best promoted. Normally we give demonstrations of our craft, one or two of us setting up inside a netted perimeter and producing a work of art in about an hour. The artist is paid a flat fee. The art, usually a bear, eagle or totem, specified by the sponsor, is auctioned as a fundraiser for the organization. Tonight, however, is an open competition. The prize purse is huge, twenty-five grand for the winner and substantial amounts for second and third. Fifteen artists from the Chainsaw Masters organization are entered along with over a half dozen renegades and wild cards from around the country. Even Barbara and Lu Anne from the Chainsaw Chix have entered. They're mostly into showmanship but Barbara can carve out a pretty decent "Barbcat" with the right piece of wood. The cool thing about tonight's performance is that we can chose to carve anything we want, no restrictions.

While Lily assembled a sandwich for me, I kicked back on the couch barely an arm's length away. Looking past her I noticed the bed made. We never do this. The space above the fifth wheel hitch that contains the sleeping quarters is too small for even Lily, at five feet tall, to stand up.

"What are you, channeling Susie Homemaker these days?" I asked. She just smiled over her shoulder.

We hadn't talked about what would happen when the season ended. My brother has a few acres outside of Biloxi where he helped me build a pad for my camper. It has all the utilities and will handle up to a double wide mobile home. I spent the last few winters there helping him with his firewood business, mostly hibernating. I hate winter.

Lily handed me the sandwich, on a plate, causing me to raise an eyebrow. She bounced down beside me.

"You're going to blow them away tonight," she said. She was aware of some of the changes to my act. She'd even suggested a couple of them. "What are you going to do with all that money?"

"I don't have any money."

"You will, after tonight."

"Well, little darlin', I thank you for your support but I am going up against over 20 of the world's best artists."

"Whatever, you'll still win. Everybody knows it." She pushed my hair back from my cheek and gave me a reassuring kiss.

"What about your buddy, Jerry?" I asked, pulling away.

"He's good, alright, but not the fancy-assed showman that you are. What you're planning has never been done before."

"Attempted."

"But not accomplished. You're the only guy I've ever met with the balls to pull that off."

"I just hope it works out. The alternative would pretty much suck."

"So do the judges know what you're planning?" She asked.

"Sshh, It's a secret." I put my finger to my lips.

"They might not go for it."

"Nothing in the rules specifically forbids it. I've been at this almost fifteen years, ever since high school, and I've never seen anyone try it."

Lily giggled. "I bet they rewrite the rules after tonight."

I still had the last bite of my sandwich in my hand when Lily tossed the plate in the sink and straddled my lap. She wrapped her arms around my neck and pressed herself against me like a second skin.

"I want to get some of this hillbilly stink all over me," she said. "Let's mess up the bed."

One thing about Lily, she was crazy wild in the sack. She liked to run the show, which was fine with me. She was good at it. Looking back, she'd always made the call, not just in the bedroom.

*****

I met Lily back in April. I was performing a demonstration behind a VFW hall in Tyler, Texas, along with one of the Chainsaw Chix named Sheila. I'd completed carving the bear I was commissioned to create. Like always, they wanted it standing on its hind legs in attack mode. I'd created dozens of these. I could pretty much carve one in my sleep. Sheila was carving an alligator, a little unusual for this part of the country, not that there weren't any gators around. Gators were usually commissioned in southern Louisiana. Sheila is a skinny girl who performs dressed in tight leather pants and matching vest over a denim work shirt. She puts her sunset red hair in a long braid under a Harley Davidson doo-rag. The perimeter of her cage was three deep in toothless meth heads. The ground was getting damp from their drool.

"Don't it bother you, all those goofballs ogling your old lady?" asked a little girl's voice. I glanced over. Lily was standing beside me sparkling with small town innocence. I just grinned and shook my head.

"First," I said, "she ain't my old lady. Her 'partner' is back at the motel and she ain't a man. Second, her girlfriend could kick any of these skinny boys' asses before they knew what hit them."

"So, where's your 'partner'?"

"I'm flying solo for now," I said.

"Really?" She looked me over head to toe like I was a used car she figured she could work a deal on. She was making me uncomfortable. She didn't look a day over fifteen. I expected a hulking brother or father to step out of the brush any minute with a shotgun aimed at my gonads. Turns out, when I pulled out of Tyler that evening Lily was riding shotgun. The only family member of hers I met was an aunt a couple of years older who was facilitating her escape. I made sure Lily was of age. She'd graduated high school the year before and attended a local community college.

"Everybody has my life planned for me," she said. "My parents, the church, but nobody asked me what I want to do. Hell, I don't even know for sure. One thing I do know is I've got to get out of this one horse town.

*****

We were all wrung out, covered in hillbilly stink and love juice, when there was a knock on the door.

"Just a minute." I pulled on some jeans and closed the curtain that serves as a door to the "bedroom."

"Hey, Jerry, come on in," I said. He had to duck to get through the door.

"The wood's here," he said. "The truck just pulled in. From where I was it looked like some good, large pieces. I'm going over to check it out. Want to come?"

"Sure, let me grab a shirt and some boots."

"Me too," Lily said from behind the curtain. I heard her bounce out of bed.

For some reason Jerry decided to befriend me. Maybe because we were favorites to win the competition. Maybe because I pretended not to be bothered that he's from New Zealand. A lot of the Masters felt he was a foreigner stealing potential gigs. He hadn't affected my bottom line. Still, our approach was different. He concentrated on artistic expression while my main goal was showmanship. He did beautiful work, very intricate and detailed. Usually, though, we didn't even get to chose what we created. We were commissioned for a particular piece that got sold and sat in the rain in front of a bar somewhere until it rotted away. I figured the crowd comes for the noise and flying wood chips. I liked to add a little cock walk, and sometimes I'd even make another larger figure then cut it away into the one I was commissioned to produce. That always got a rise out of the crowd..

When we reached the racetrack, the infield was already divided by chalk lines into 24 squares. There were two officials on hand. The other competitors began to gather. I picked a square near the center and let an official know of my preference. Jerry picked an adjoining square. The wood was perfect; oak and pecan, green cut and oozing sap, exactly what I needed to make my plan work. I picked out a tall oak trunk with a slight bend in it. Jerry picked a shorter stump with a large diameter. I knew it would be pointless to ask him what he planned to carve. He would no more tell me his plan than I would tell him mine.

Jacksonville, Florida is a port city. I'll admit that factored into my choice of sculpture. Once our chosen chunks of wood were fork lifted into our preferred workspace, we left. Workers would erect fishnet cages around each piece leaving room for the crowd to circulate among the competitors.

"Let's grab a beer and head over to the livestock arena," Jerry suggested. "The sheep finals start in a few minutes."

I couldn't have cared less about sheep.

"Cool!" Lily said. "Sounds like fun."

"Sure," I said.

We were about halfway through our pints of warm beer and I'd had about all I could take of listening to Jerry pontificate about the merits of various sheep breeds when he turned to me.

"Why don't you two come to New Zealand when the season ends?" He asked. "We have chainsaw art opportunities down under. There aren't as many but they pay better. We could use a showman like you to liven things up."

"I don't know. I'm kind of obligated to help my brother with his firewood business. Besides, where would we live?"

"My family has a ranch. We have plenty of room. I'm sure they'd be fine with you staying if you helped out with the stock. You're both welcome to come. New Zealand is a beautiful place."

"I don't know. I can't see it happening, but who knows?"

"Think about it," Jerry said. "I'll go get us another beer."

As soon as Jerry was out of earshot, Lily was all over it. "How cool is that! Travel to another country! Let's do it!"

"I'm supposed to help my brother this winter," I said. "He set me up with a pad and utilities. I can't just bail on him. I don't see it happening. I don't even have a passport."

"Me either, but we could get one. All you need is a birth certificate and an ID. You can even push it through quick for a few extra bucks. C'mon, it'll be fun." She was pulling on my sleeve like she was ready to leave that instant.

"I doubt it. We'll be in Biloxi for the winter. Winter's short here anyway."

She stuck her lip out like a five year old and her eyes burned with disappointment. She folded her arms over her chest and refused to look at me. Jerry returned with the beer and sat down on the other side of Lily.

"So what about it?" He asked.

"We'll see," I said. Attentions returned to sheep. Enthusiasm was dampened.

*****

Carneys, hawkers and gypsy traders, awakened by the poisoned blood coursing through their veins, analyzed their marks. Local heroes, innocent victims of their egos, prepared to impress their friends and families with prowess at the unwinnable games of the midway. The crowds thickened. The smells intensified. The setting sun projected vibrant colors onto the heavy cloud bank building to the west. Occasional flashes of orange and blue reflected from behind the horizon. I hoped the rain would hold off until after the competition. A storm could ruin my plan.

I was dressed in my pearl snap shirt, black jeans, boots, leather vest and chaps. Lily braided my hair into a single thick rope down my back. All of her sassy playfulness had vanished. I figured I could redeem myself with a win tonight. Even if not, my chosen sculpture was sure to impress her.

I carried the two saws I normally used; the eighteen-inch bar for the rough cuts and the ten-inch narrow bar with the lightweight power head for detail work. Lily carried the gas can and the special unit I had modified for tonight's performance. The power head was painted gloss black. The fourteen inch bar was chrome plated and polished to a mirror finish.. The major modification, however, wasn't visible to the naked eye. I enlarged the orifice from the bar oiler. Instead of heavyweight bar oil, I'd filled the reservoir with used motor oil mixed with a generous amount of 200 proof grain alcohol.

Once the artists were enclosed in their protective netting the announcer came over the P.A. He went over the basic rules and safety precautions for spectators. His final announcement, predictable, being that it was the deep South, was "Gentlemen start your engines".

I glanced over at Jerry. He walked around in a circle, cocking his head from side to side, but the crowd was already too thick for me to see his stump. I started the large saw and looked at my tree trunk. I could see the mermaid inside. I only needed to set her free. She was tall and lean but the woman half of her body was Lily's twin. I pranced around the tree a couple of times, revving the saw, getting the crowd's attention. I cut several large chunks free and kicked them toward the perimeter.

Half an hour later, the mermaid appeared, though she was rough and angular. I picked up the small saw and gave form to the tail fin. I softened her facial features and shaped her arms, hands and fingers. She was looking pretty good. I put curl and texture to the hair that cascaded over her shoulders. Time for the show, I started the "special" saw. Very little wood was being taken away now. That wasn't the point. What was happening was that the fish half of the statue, her hair and bikini top were being coated with the oil/alcohol mix. That done, I reached in my pocket, flipped open my lighter and held it to the tip of the tailfin. A flick of the thumb and the mermaid was engulfed in a flame the color of offshore open water. A collective gasp rose from the crowd as they moved closer. The flames reflected off the chrome bar, flashing beams of blue light into the wanton eyes of the spectators. Revving the saw was like a psychedelic flame thrower aimed at the base of the statue. Each rev of the saw brought a cheer from the growing audience. The alcohol burned away quickly and the oil in the mix left a sienna sheen to the surface of the sculpture as it burned away more slowly. I strutted around the perimeter of the enclosure, shooting columns of blue flame into the sky while the combustibles on the mermaid burned away. The chocolate colored residue allowed for shading. When the flames died back I started the small saw again and used the flat side of the bar's tip to create the illusion of scales on the mermaid's tail. I added highlights to the woman's darkened hair. I fine tuned the details of the facial features, shoulders and torso of the woman. Feeling that I could make no further improvements to the work, I took the two unmodified chainsaws, one in each hand, and, spinning like a top, saws outstretched, I carved the title of the work in the base; "Lily Of The Sea". I held the saws above my head revving them alternately. The crowd roared. It's what I lived for.

I wasn't the first artist finished but I was by far not the last. I stepped from the enclosure and saw Lily a few feet away. I sidled up to her and took her hand. She was radiant.

"God, that's incredible!" She said. "I've never seen anything like it. I'm totally amazed."

"Thanks," I said. "I had so much fun. I didn't know if I could pull it off but it all came together. Let's take a look around at the competition."

There were a lot of animals; bears, wildcats, eagles. A couple of guys made cigar store Indians. There was one modern art type of sculpture by a guy I'd never heard of. I wondered how well that would fly with the county fair crowd. One big surprise was Lu Anne from the Chainsaw Chix. I'd never seen her produce anything that impressed me. Today, though, she dressed in a tight pink leather outfit. She'd painted her saws pink and even her hair was dyed pink. She produced a very accurate likeness of herself riding a Harley chopper, hair blowing back in the wind. The bike was set at an angle as if accelerating through a curve. The work had an aura of motion. She titled it "Self Portrait." As we approached she was just wrapping up the detail work.

"That's pretty damn good!" I said. "I might have something to worry about here." Her perimeter was several feet deep in horny young men cheering every time she bent to touch up a low part of the sculpture. When she finished she blew kisses to the crowd.

"Classy!" Lily said.

"Yeah, she definitely caught me by surprise. I bet she takes home some prize money."

"Let's go check out Jerry's work," Lily said.

That tight spot in me started burning. "Sure, whatever."

"Don't be that way," Lily scolded. "He's nice. He wants to be our friend. What's wrong with that? He even offered us a place to stay when we go to New Zealand."

"If," I corrected. Her eyes rolled.

As we neared his enclosure he was wiping down his saws with a red shop rag. He then took a whisk broom and gently brushed the wood chips and sawdust from the sculpture. I'd have to say, without a doubt, Jerry does the most detailed work of any chainsaw artist I've seen. Although we were approaching from behind, this seemed intricate even for him. It was a woman sitting in a patch of rain lilies. She was leaning on one hand with her feet pulled up beside her. The other hand was outstretched holding a nut toward a bushy tailed squirrel. The woman's curly hair tumbled down her shoulders. As we walked around to the front of his creation my heart stuck in my throat. The detail was such that I didn't need to see the title to know. I was unsure of how to react so I didn't. I just looked at the title, "Lily With Lilies", and quit breathing. I looked up quick enough to see their eyes meet.

They didn't even notice me. I looked at the ground and noticed a battery operated grinder. That explained the foliage. No one could carve rain lilies with that much detail using a chain saw, no matter how talented they were. I took Lily by the arm, breaking into their conversation. "I need you to give me a hand," I said, pulling her away.

"I'll see you later," Jerry said, smiling. I wasn't sure who he was talking to. At this point, I no longer had anything to say to him.

"Grab that saw," I told Lily. "We need to get packed up before this storm hits." The wind had already begun to blow dust across the infield. As I was leaving I found one of the officials.

"You need to check out our 'mate' over by the squirrel feeder," I said. "I think you'll find he used some unauthorized equipment."

Lily planted herself in front of me holding my chainsaw between us. Her feet were set squarely and her nostrils flared. "What the fuck are you doing. Jerry is our friend. You're being a major asshole."

"He's not my friend," I said. "My friends play by the rules."

She dropped my saw in the dirt and stomped off toward the trailer. I picked up the saw but I couldn't carry all three saws and the gas can. I took the valuables. I could always get another can. I got to the trailer but Lily wasn't there. She needed time to cool off, I figured. She had to realize that there was too much at stake here to let somebody get away with cheating. I packed my saws away and retracted the awning so it didn't get damaged by the wind. After waiting a few minutes for Lily, I decided to go see how the judging was going. Blue fingers of lightning were dancing across the western horizon. We needed to be battened down soon, inside and comfortable.

They were announcing the winners just as I got back to the infield. The guy with the modern art sculpture won third place. *"Well, I'll be damned!"* I thought. Second prize went to Lu Anne. *"Good for her."* When they announced first prize I nearly dropped to my knees. I'd won. I couldn't wait to tell Lily. I ran back to the trailer, no Lily, but her clothes and toiletries were gone. She left a brief note.

I had no idea how mean you could be. I'm going to New Zealand. See you next year,- maybe.   -Lily

Stunned would have been an understatement. I sat at the table and read the note over and over until a booming clap of thunder shook the trailer. I pulled on my coat and went to the business office to collect my prize. They congratulated me. I thanked them. They asked if I could stop by the next day when it was light for a picture with my sculpture.

"Sure," I said.

I hooked up my trailer and stuck the check in the glove compartment of the truck. I took one last walk over to the infield.

The crowd had dispersed. The wind was howling now and every flash of lightning made me twitch. The mermaid stood tall against the other sculptures. I looked again at Jerry's work. I had to admit he had a unique eye for detail. He'd captured a part of Lily that I'd never noticed. I remembered the gas can I'd left in the field. Yep, it was still there. Might as well use it.

Just as I pulled out of the exhibitor's area, large drops of rain began pounding against the windshield. The gale had blown over one of the ficus trees I left in the parking lot. In the rearview, I could see flames licking up skyward as the lightning split the air. It reminded me of a dance. The flashing lights from the fire trucks were about to cut in.

*****

I slowly advanced up my brother's driveway and looped behind the house to center the camper on the concrete pad. I didn't call ahead. I didn't even know if he was home. I was about to disconnect from the trailer when I heard the screen door slam. He came toward me in jeans and house shoes. The air seemed a bit brisk to go shirtless. Maybe it was just me.

"Welcome home," he yelled across the yard. "I hear you hit the jackpot, you high roller."

"I guess," I replied.

"So where's this Lily I've been hearing so much about?"

"Long story," I said. I hate winter.

BONNEVILLE

Roscoe found God at 436.8 miles per hour.

"We've got a baby coming, you dickhead!" Shirleen's words echoed in his mind when the right rear tire blew. Over a dozen 360° spirals later he drug his vomit covered body from the intact vehicle. Ten years later he still held true to his promise. Shirleen was dust in the wind like pretty much every other woman he'd encountered, But Casey? Casey was a keeper. If Roscoe had one good thing in his life it was his son.

"A promise is a promise" was something his dad had spouted pretty regular, words being easy and all. Roscoe's dad left little pieces like that strung behind him. Roscoe was one. When it's God, though, shouldn't that mean something? No matter how much the owners cajoled him, he never stepped into the cockpit of another race car. Rumors abounded that he had lost his nerve. Maybe. He had definitely lost his need for speed.

Casey terrified Roscoe. Some kind of genetics had to be working there. When Casey went to his first carnival at four years old, he darted right past the merry-go-round to the little fiberglass cars with numbers on the side. A couple of years later it was bumper cars.

"Please, daddy, drive me, please!" His little eyes shined like blue steel bearings, spinning Roscoe back to his childhood. "Just one time, Daddy, can you let me drive it?"

It wasn't but a few years later he ran across Mona, not really his type, but he was intrigued. Her name fit her so well. It damn sure wasn't love at first sight.

Roscoe could give up racing but even God knew better than to ask him to give up cars altogether. He fit right in at the car rental agency. His brush with fame didn't hurt, having taken a shot at the land speed record. It wasn't long before the entry level grunt managed his own branch of the agency. The money was okay. The perks were outstanding. The best part about it was the travel. The company was okay with him taking his son along on transfers when one of their specialty cars went to a satellite branch.

They were loaded up with pork rinds and Dr. Pepper on Highway 7 southbound from Fayetteville, Arkansas after switching the Lamborghini for a Hyundai Accent. Casey was still pumped.

"Dad, why didn't you open that baby up when we had it. I know it'll break 200. I Googled it."

"My job maybe, the thing that buys the pork rinds which, by the way, are perfectly okay to eat in this Hyundai."

"How fast will this car go?"

"Fast enough to get a ticket. You have to be on the racetrack to race."

Casey seized up. But not enough to keep him from scarfing down most of the pig skins, and not for long.

"Dad, check that out! We've got to stop!"

Roscoe had let the tight curves of the mountain road take him back to another time. He'd failed to notice the handwritten plywood sign stating "Fastest Go Karts in Arkansas" leaning against a barbed wire fence, but Casey was on it."It's a racetrack, Dad! You said, remember? I'll race you!"

It's interesting how the rules get interpreted, but Roscoe had a lifetime of experience with this. "I didn't say we *would* race, just that you had to be on a racetrack."

"So can we?" Casey was unfazed.

"Whatever," Roscoe's said. He needed a pee break anyway. "If they're open." It was only go-karts, how bad could it be? He pulled into the red dirt drive, past the ancient, pine tree sequestered Airstream and parked by a converted stable. An asphalt track had been cut through the woods and piles of old tires lined the turns. As Roscoe was preparing to declare it a death trap, he heard the door of the Airstream slap shut. The woman who ambled toward him wore jeans stuck partway down in square toed boots, a black biker tee shirt and a large caliber pistol that hung low on her rather wide hips. A red doo-rag held back hair that cascaded down her shoulders like rivulets of used motor oil. Latina? Native American? Gypsy? Roscoe wasn't sure. It didn't really matter.

"Hey boys, y'all wanting to drive 'em?" Her accent had a Cajun flavor.

"Maybe," Roscoe said, "What's the deal?"

"Five bucks each plus a dollar a lap. You sign this release. I fire 'em up." She pulled some folded papers from her hip pocket. "I'm Mona by the way."

"I'm Roscoe and this little guy is Casey."

Casey shot his dad an angry glance. "I'm almost 10."

"He'll be nine next month. Probably he'll need to ride with me."

"Your call, you sign, you drive. If you can reach the peddles, you're in."

"So, how can you advertise the fastest cars?"

"My brother built these back in the eighties. Some German rotary engines he picked up called a Wankel. They have a wide power band and a shitload of torque. Clocked 'em at 75 over straight road. See that electronic timer on the back straightaway? It's got radar. Couple local guys can break 50 on that little chunk of track. That's pretty damn fast when you're 2 inches off the ground."

"That sounds a little extreme for a kid." Roscoe got that look again.

"We got helmets."

"See, Dad, we'll be fine. We've got to do this. We might never get another chance. Besides, you wouldn't even open up the Lamborghini."

If y'all have a Lambo this might be a little tame," Mona said.

"It's not mine. I just delivered it," Roscoe said. He looked over the legalese with a furrowed brow.

"All that means is if you end up dead or dismembered my brother or me don't get sued."

"I doubt this is binding."

"Maybe not, you still got to sign it. He's already in jail and if you look around there ain't much point in suing me."

"What about insurance?" Roscoe asked.

Mona snorted. "Maybe y'all ought to just forget it."

Casey saw the deal heading south. "Come on, Dad. I'll be careful. You can pace me."

"You got a bathroom?" Roscoe asked as he pulled out his wallet.

"In the trailer, but you can just pee behind the barn if that's all you need." She took the money. They headed for opposite sides of the barn.

When Roscoe came back around to the business side of the building he saw a few dozen flat pan carts in various stages of disassembly. Half a dozen were in the pit area. Mona pushed a couple onto the track, checked the fuel and started them with a pull rope. "Gas on the right, brake on the left," she said. "Let 'em warm up for a minute then y'all can have a free practice lap" She turned on the scoreboard. "You know, Roscoe, you look real familiar to me. Could I know you?"

"I doubt it. I manage a car rental agency in northwest Houston. I have one of those faces I guess. I get that a lot."

The car was the perfect size for Casey. Roscoe had to stuff himself in. He took a practice lap with Casey hugging his bumper. The machine did have some balls. When he punched it coming out of turn four onto the straightaway, the drive wheels broke traction. His first official lap the radar read 38 miles per hour. Casey was still on his bumper. An increase in heart rate was pounding the adrenaline through his body. He held tight in the groove on the turns making sure that Casey couldn't squeeze by but allowed a little freedom on the straightaway. The little Wankels were singing harmony, 43 miles per hour on lap three. Casey was pumped too. Roscoe took turn one wide coming out of the straits and Casey almost slipped inside. Roscoe panicked and broke traction but darted back in the lead at turn two. *So this is how it's going to be,* Roscoe thought. He braked checked Casey causing them to tap bumpers. He heard an explosion. When he looked over he saw Mona with her pistol in the air, shaking a finger at them. They both backed off. Lap three's speed on the straight was only 32. Mona folded her arms. Roscoe kept the turn tight coming out of the straight but Casey fishtailed around the outside and gunned it for the sweet spot in turn two. The kid came in low, but too fast, and went into a skid. Genetics took over. He turned into it. Although he clipped the barrier, knocking a couple of used tires into the woods, he pulled ahead and was gone. Roscoe spent the rest of the six laps trying to catch up, ending 1/2 lap behind. When he came into the final straightaway the realized that the 58 miles per hour that flashed on the radar board wasn't him.

Roscoe extricated himself from the little machine while Casey spun around him in a victory dance.

"The kid dusted your ass," Mona said. "He set a new track record by 4 miles per hour. You've got a driver here."

Roscoe's fingers were still tingling from gripping the steering wheel as Mona handed Casey an honest to God checkered flag. "Can I get his picture by the scoreboard? These hillbillies around here ain't going to believe this kid out raced them."

"What the hell was that with the pistol?" Roscoe's mind was on other things. "You could have killed one of us!"

"Not with blanks." Mona held the pistol out for Roscoe's examination."Let me fix y'all some dinner. I've got some boudin from last time Mama came up. Besides, I done figured out where I know you from."

A man sized portion of the spicy sausage and rice left Casey's head lolling towards the arm of Mona's couch. The sun was giving way.

"We better get going, but thanks for the meal. I've still got some miles to go," Roscoe's said.

Mona shook her finger at him."Nonsense, that couch makes into a bed. You'd have to stop somewhere anyway."

Roscoe saw that Casey had given in to the sandman. "I'd never argue with a woman packing heat."

"Good. I want to show you something anyway." She went to the back of the trailer and came back with blankets and a tattered scrapbook bulging with yellowed newspaper clippings."My daddy was a flat track racer on the Gulf Coast circuit. They called him the Dirt Track Demon. I was nine when he ate a wall. My brother was 13. He really took it hard. Me too, I reckon. Mama collected up all the news clippings she could find and stuck 'em in here. My brother added just about everything he could find on racing and fast cars. He tried to race but I think Daddy dying like that made him skittish. Not me though, I was like Daddy. He always said 'It's better to flame out than get old and decrepit.' I like speed but they didn't let girls race when I was coming up. It's kind of late to start now." She plopped down on the sagging couch and motioned Roscoe to join her. When she opened the scrapbook it caught Casey's attention too. She pointed out a few highlights of her dad's career then flipped toward the back of the book. "So, who's this guy?"

Roscoe was looking at a younger, thinner version of himself sporting a black mustache and a red, white and blue fire suit. He was standing on the Bonneville salt flats next to the American Arrow, the vehicle he had long ago sprayed with his gastric juices. The caption left nothing to the imagination.

Casey was wide awake now. "Holy crap, Dad, is that you?"

"That was before you were born."

"But, Dad, the land speed record? Shit, that's awesome!"

"Language, son. There's a lady present."

Mona snorted. "That's your dad. You didn't know?"

"Look, that's old news. I never thought it was important."

"It's the land speed record!" Mona and Casey said in unison.

"I didn't break it. I didn't even come close, plus, I nearly died."

"Better to flame out." Mona said.

Casey read the caption again. "437 miles per hour! Oh my god! That must have been awesome."

"I guess I thought so at the time."

They looked at a few more clippings related to the Bonneville salt flats. It was a couple of years later before the record was broken and the American Arrow had been retired by then. Mona pulled out the couch so Casey could stretch out while the adults sat at the kitchen table drinking beer and telling racing stories. Around midnight, when Roscoe excused himself, Mona grabbed his hand. "It's more comfortable back here," she said, nodding toward the bedroom.

"What about Casey?"

"He's not invited."

"No, I mean ..."

"I'm not going to tell and you're obviously pretty good at secrets." Mona looked good through his beer stained eyes. He craved being tangled in those long black locks.

Like most of the women he'd been with, she took control of the situation. Like very few of the women he'd been with, she took great pleasure in the endeavor. Somewhere beyond exhaustion he put on some of his clothes and stumbled back to the couch.

The boys wakened to the smell of drop biscuits and homemade ham gravy. "Before y'all head out I was hoping to let Casey on the track solo so he could take a crack at his own record without any interference," Mona said.

The glaze of sleep vanished from Casey's eyes. Roscoe was uncommonly pliable. "Sure."

"Then I want to race you," she said. Her dark eyes spun him around. He'd have agreed to anything.

"Sounds like fun." He dug into breakfast with an unnatural hunger.

*****

Casey broke 50 miles per hour on four of his five laps but never matched the 58 from the previous day. Something about human competition? Maybe.

Mona and Roscoe lined up side by side to start. Mona had the pole, her track. She got the jump on him and it was into the second lap before he had his chance. She was riding the sweet spot when he came in from behind, high and outside. He punched it and nosed to the inside, tight between her and the rail. Just as he passed he broke traction and slid toward the wall, almost clipping her front bumper. She nosed inside but he kept the pressure on and had her by half a length when they cleared the curve. He never gained much more. They screamed through the straight at 54 with her jockeying for the inside. He pinched her out. She tried pulling around the outside but he was deep in the groove.

On the final lap he rode a couple of the turns high. She easily snuck inside and took the lead but he was on her back door in the straight, screaming at 56 miles per hour.

She took a victory lap. Casey gave her temporary custody of the flag. She stomped toward Roscoe.

"You suck! That was some sorry-ass shit! I didn't ask for that. You don't throw a race. What sort of message is that for Casey?"

"Hey, we're just having fun here."

"I don't *need* to beat you. I don't *need* anything at all from you. Just get out of here!"

"Hey, easy!"

"Leave now! Get your shit and go. I can't believe I... I overestimated you." She spun on her heel and stomped off, slamming the door behind her.

"I guess we should go," Roscoe told his son. Casey rolled the flag around the stick as they got in the Hyundai.

Miles of silence passed before Casey asked, "What was that all about. I thought you guys were getting along great."

"I screwed up. I let her win. You never know with women, at least I don't."

*****

It was four months before Roscoe finagled a trip up Highway 7 again. The trailer was there but the sign was gone. He pulled in the driveway and found the track grown up with weeds. The pickup she drove was still there. A man with a gold earring and a spider web tattoo on his neck stood in the doorway.

"Is Mona around?" Roscoe asked.

"Nope."

"Do you know when she'll be back?"

"Nope."

"Can you tell her Ros...."

"I know who you are. She moved back to Louisiana to take care of some family business."

"So you must be her brother."

"Yup."

"Can you tell me how to reach her?"

"Nope, but I'll tell you what, next time I talk to her I'll tell her you came by."

"Cool, here's my card."

Spidcrwcb snorted and took the card. "Card, huh? Figures." The door closed, a bit more forcefully than was necessary.

*****

The next spring Roscoe was going over first quarter receipts when his assistant came in. "Sir, a woman out here wants to rent the Lamborghini," she said.

"Lambo's out."

"I told her that but she wants to talk to you."

"I can't do anything. It's due back Monday."

"I told her. She wants to see you. She asked for you by name."

Roscoe exhaled. "Fine, tell her I'll be out in a minute."

"She's dressed like money."

"Okay, okay, just a minute."

The hips gave shape to the little black dress but the large hat and Ray Bans threw him for a minute.

"My brother says you're looking for me," Mona said. Her full lips were not smiling. Her hands were supported by those fabulous hips.

"Yeah," he swallowed as his employees froze in place. "I am, I mean, I was. I mean... hey."

Mona shook her head. "Still the silver-tongued devil, I see." She opened her arms. "How about a hug."

Roscoe stepped into her arms and whispered, "Does this mean we're okay?"

"We'll see. What about that Lambo?"

"Next week?"

"I'll be in Daytona next week. What else you got, and don't try to put me in no Hyundai."

"Best I can do is an LT3 Corvette."

"I never drove one. Can you come with me and show me how?"

"What, to Daytona?"

"Yeah, but I'm driving."

LEAKER

Lately, when I'm dreaming, I dream blood is leaking out of my body. I find that disturbing. It's not that a lot of blood leaks out. It's that it always leaks out in some manner it's leaked out in the past. I've always had vivid dreams – color, smell, taste, sound – all the senses. It made for some really interesting dreams earlier in my life but now that I'm into my second half century I don't get the erotic dreams as often, just these blood leakers and dreams about my job. In the "leakers" I rarely lose much blood and I'm never close to death or anything. It's always something like dropping my Harley on a gravel road, sliding off a pipe rack or slicing my thumb with a hunting knife. The other night I dreamed I shot some crank. The needle broke from the syringe and blood started squirting out. I woke up with my heart beating fast, rushing as if I'd actually done a shot. I couldn't get back to sleep so I washed my bike and polished the chrome, laughing at the money I'd saved.

Thursday is the Fourth. The guys with jobs, like me, are taking off Friday to enjoy our summer run. I hoped to convince everybody to go inland to the Hill Country or the Piney Woods but everyone wanted to go to the beach. Hell, we all live within 50 miles of the damn beach. We go to the beach almost every weekend in the summer. So instead of Surfside, like we always do, I talked them in to South Padre so we can get some road time.

Things are a little out of whack. I've been up since last Friday getting my bike ready. I raked the frame 4 degrees and installed the springer forks Gypsy bought me for my birthday last month. It's 8 inches over stock, bringing the front end up a bit high. A smaller front wheel leveled it out. Now it's a long, lean, old school chopper. I took my Fat Boy tank over to Flash. He painted it gloss black with these blood red veins running all through it, even shading them to look raised from the surface. My scooter looks good!

I've been president of the One Percenters Motorcycle Club for eleven years, mostly because all the guys get along. In addition to being voted to replace me as President, anyone elected would have to physically remove the patch from my colors. Not gonna happen, not because I'm the biggest. Bear is. He tried to take my place four years ago. He ended up with 38 stitches and nearly lost a kidney. I'm glad he's okay now. He's a bad ass and really handy to have around when you need to deal with the cops. He's an ex-cop and doesn't drink or do any drugs, except pot, so he can usually keep his head. I guess I'm the oldest next to Bear and maybe Mondo. Nobody knows how old he is, probably not even him. It'll sure be good to ride with Mondo again. He's been up country a while. He got ten years after being popped for knocking over a drug store. He did about four and a half and they let him out for – well, who knows – but he's out. I think Mondo getting' locked up might be what set off Bear wanting to be President. We're the last three of the original One Percenters.

"Roman! Dinner's getting cold. You need to eat. Life resumes tomorrow,"

"That's my ole lady, "Gypsy". She must be pissed or she wouldn't use my given name.

"I'll eat later. I've got to get these damn LEDs working. They keep blowing fuses."

"Shit, Wolf, when is the last time you slept? Maybe you ought to put it away and look at it with a fresh head later. Come get fed. I got a couple of blues that will put you in Dreamland."

See how she is. Always trying to be my wet nurse. I pulled her out of a bad spot when she was about 16. Her mama would have put the cops on me but I said to leave us alone or I'd put 'em right back on her step-dad after I fed him his balls. Better than 25 years later and she's still around. A lot of the women running with us tend to get a little rough over the years, but not Gypsy. She's still as thin and sharp as a switchblade knife. Barely any gray in her jet black hair and those steel blue eyes can burn right through you. Hell, she gets her leather on and even the young guys start getting stupid over her. She's mine. Being President, I don't share.

*****

Damn it was hot! Must have been after midnight. No breeze coming off the Gulf, just the smell of rotting seaweed, dead fish and petroleum products. The breakers looked like electricity arcing across the top of the waves in the moonlight. Soggy air. Silhouettes of salt grass sprung from the dunes like thousands of sharp, black needles. How long had I been sitting here? Everybody gone. Shaggy was cleaning up, too late for last call.

"You okay?" It was Shaggy.

"Yeah, just tired."

"Well, you can sit here all night if you want. If you leave, turn off the light over the bar. Leave on the light over the pool table, lock up and go out the back."

"Sure, later."

From here on the deck you could see about a quarter mile of beach, deserted this far down. Shaggy's old Econoline steered through the dunes out onto the beach road, the one working taillight fading into the damp night.

"Hey, Wolf, you still alive out here?"

"What? Oh, Stella, I thought everybody left."

"I guess you thought wrong. One body is still here."

Stella sat down right next to my empty bottle, took off her pink gimme cap and tossed it to the other end of the table. Her dark blonde hair dropped down passed her shoulders, partially covering her brown eyes.

She leaned in toward my face. "I didn't want you to have to clean up after yourself." Her smoky Southern voice as smooth as Kentucky bourbon.

"So you're here for my empties"

"I'm here for whatever you need." She leaned back, stretching out on the long table. "You're the boss."

I have to admit I hadn't thought of Stella that way in a while. I'd known her a couple of years. She's Shaggy's loud mouth, smart assed bartender, and his oldest daughter. Yeah, she looked damned sweet but she's at least 20 years younger than me. *What the hell!* I grabbed her behind the neck with one hand and slid my other hand up between her thighs, just below her blue jean cutoffs. I pulled her from the table onto my lap, knocking my empty bottle to the ground. I pressed my mouth hard onto hers. As her lips parted, I thrust my tongue in. My hand slipped up to the crotch of her cutoffs and I felt a damp warmth intensify my interest. I caught my breath. "Maybe I should toss you up on that pool table so you don't get splinters in that sweet little ass of yours."

~ 182 ~

"Yeah, somethin' like that might work!" she panted.

Once inside she turned and pressed firmly against me, engaging in one more deep wet kiss.

"Sit!" she motioned toward a wooden chair. I sat. She straddled my left leg with her beautiful heart shaped butt towards me and pulled my shin up, grabbing it between her thighs. She began working my boot slowly back and forth. "A little help here?"

I pressed my other boot up against her butt as she wiggled the first one loose. Gently releasing my leg, she straddled the other foot and we repeated the procedure. She picked up the boots and placed them on a nearby chair then leaned against the pool table. She shimmied out of those tiny cutoffs revealing nothing but creamy white skin and a small patch of glistening, golden fleece. I was already breathing hard and grabbing at my clothes as she pulled her t-shirt over her head, tossing it against the wall. Her long golden hair fell gently down framing her erect pink nipples with the chrome studs through them.

"Did that hurt?" I asked while gently fingering one of the tiny barbells.

"Oh yeah, quite beautifully!" she recalled and grabbed my hand, forcing me to pinch her very firmly. "You lie down on that table, Boss. I have a special treat for you. I've been practicing."

Not one to squelch youthful creativity, I finished undressing and stretched out on the table, placing my hands behind my head, my maypole dancing in the spotlight. She hopped up on the table and straddled me, dripping with anticipation.

"You're not in a hurry are you?" she asked.

"I've got all night."

Once united, she began grinding and writhing slowly forward and backward, up and down, her hands full of my furry gray chest hair. She arched her back and beads of sweat formed on her neck and breasts. As the first rivulets slid down her cheeks she began to tremble and a low moan shook her body. Still she rocked slowly back and forth as her hands tensed and pulled hard at my chest hair. The first drops of perspiration dripped from her nipples, turning to a dark blood red liquid as it fell to my throat. She moaned again, grinding harder and slower, throwing back her damp hair and showering me with droplets of the red juice. I closed my eyes, trying to make the ecstasy last. When I opened my eyes it was Gypsy slowly riding me. She stared down at me in anger as she intently carved into my chest with my hunting knife. The pain was overtaking the pleasure. Blood was pooling on my chest along with a generous smear of black tattoo ink.

"Bitch! What are you doing?!"

"Making sure you know God-damned well that your mine. This is my name – big, deep letters!" she cackled, slamming her pelvis hard against mine, groaning and shuddering, teeth barred.

"Get off me, bitch!" I grabbed her by the face and threw her to the floor. Jumping off the table I stumbled.

I awoke on my knees in my bedroom. Gypsy sprawled in front of her dresser rubbing a bump on her forehead with a skinned hand.

"Breakfast is ready," she said, her ice blue eyes glaring.

"Oh shit! I'm sorry, Baby. I must have been having a bad dream."

"Yeah, so I gathered." She got up and left the room.

I dressed while my erection faded. "I'm screwed now," I figure.

I sat down at the table where two large potato and egg tacos waited, along with a side of crisp bacon. The coffee was hot. Gypsy was cold. We ate in silence as I watched the knot on her forehead change from red to blue. She finished her breakfast and looked at me, trying for some insight.

"You've been twisted a little tight lately." It wasn't a question.

I said nothing. She watched me closely, waiting for my next move. I finished my coffee.

"Want some more?" she asked.

"No, I've got to get to work."

"Can't we talk?"

I figured that was coming. "Maybe later."

"Later might be too late"

"I really have to go. I'll be late."

"Mondo called. He's stopping by this evening."

"Cool, It'll be good to see him again."

"Wolf?"

"Yeah?"

"I love you but you've got to chill. This is getting weird."

"I know."

*****

Work sucked, like everybody knew about something bad happening, but they weren't talking. Traffic sucked. The kids in their lowrider trucks getting ready to party, not giving a shit about other people on the road. Pulling into my driveway felt like a deep breath.

Gypsy sat on the porch sipping a longneck. Beside her sat a guy that looked vaguely like Mondo, forty pounds heavier and a lot grayer. He jumped up when I got out of the truck.

"Wolf, you old son of a bitch, how you doin', bro?!" He gave me a rough hug.

"Damn, I see they fed you good. My tax dollars at work!" I said, glad to see my old compadre. Gypsy popped open a cold longneck and handed it to me.

"How was work?" She asked.

"Sucked, as usual. Glad to see your sweet ass!"

"You too," she said, swatting my butt." Kick back and chill. I'll go twist one."

"I can't." Mondo said. "I'm on parole and I'm pretty sure they're gonna be piss testing me about every fifteen minutes."

"That's okay," I said." I've got some crank. It'll wash out of your system in 24 hours. Let's do a line and watch the sunrise?"

Gypsy turned on me. "Shit, Wolf, can't you just leave it alone. I've got enchiladas in the oven. Save it for the weekend."

"I'm holding out for the enchiladas!" Mondo said.

I had to say something. "Yeah, you don't look like you miss many meals," Mondo just grinned.

Sometimes Gypsy pisses me off, trying to run my life. She thinks I can't handle it. I played this game when she still played with her Barbies.

"So, Mondo, Did you get up with Cherokee since you've been out?" I said. "I hear you're a daddy."

"Naw, word is, she's bartending or dancing or whatever up on Telephone road. She used to visit every now and then about the first year I was in. If that's my baby, she had the first 15 month pregnancy on record."

Gypsy laughed. "Yeah, we figured the numbers and it didn't work out."

"So, y'all getting back together?" I asked.

"Aint part of my plan, I'll keep my free agent status for now!" Mondo grinned.

"Well you're coming on the summer run. There's always the beach girls," I said.

"Hell yeah! I'm definitely looking forward to that. I've got enough saved up for at least a dozen of those fliptails."

"Fuckin' men! Talkin' shit!" Gypsy chuckled. "I better get my ass in the kitchen 'fore I have to set you boys straight. You best be hungry. We're looking at about ten minutes."

"Don't let the screen door hit your butt." I waved her off.

Mondo and I sat quietly for a minute watching a squirrel romp around in the pecan tree. He looked at me without his usual goofy grin. "Seriously, Bro, you alright? You're old lady's worried about you, man. She thinks you're spending too much time with the wizard. Maybe y'all ought to take a break and get away for awhile."

"I can't believe that bitch put our business on the street!" I was livid.

"Whoa, Wolf! I'm not the street. I'm your Bro. We go way back. She's just worried about you. You've got to admit you are looking pretty rung out."

"Well let me tell you something. Life ain't easy out here on the economy, but I damn sure have it handled. Look around. I just about have this place paid off. That '56 Chevy pickup in there looks like it just rolled off the showroom floor and my ole lady can dress any damn way she pleases. I don't see a problem!"

"Sometimes it ain't about stuff," he said, like he ain't been getting' his three squares.

"Just let it go, Mondo. I'm cool." I really need to change the subject. Mondo senses it too.

"So what's the plan for the weekend run?" He asked.

"Everybody meets here around 10 Thursday morning. Gypsy's taking the Chevy to haul our supplies. That's why my scooter has the butt bucket instead of her queen seat. Psycho's recent squeeze is gonna ride with her. That's Naomi, a wild bitch that's been kind of passed around. She dances down at the Wild Rose. Shaggy's supplying refreshments. He's actually breaking his old Goldwing out of mothballs to ride with us. I guess Stella will keep the bar open while he's gone. Then there's Jack and Leland, You know them, and Bruce. He fell into some cash when his dad died. He bought the Harley franchise in Angleton. Lucky bastard. Lucky for us too, we get good discounts. Helen ain't with him no more. She's running a shell shop and surfboard rental place down on Quintana. Bruce has a new squeeze but she ain't coming. We have a couple of prospects, kid named T-Bone, swears he's 21 but looks about 18. He rides a Sporty. His buddy, Greg, rides a stock rice burner but he packs some kick-ass pot. T-Bone's bringing his ole lady, Patty, but I seriously doubt she'll see much action. She's ugly as a mud fence and 200 plus pounds. Then you've got Roby, still riding that Norton. There's June, he's riding solo. A couple of the beach girls from Shaggy's said that they might follow us down. We'll see. Bear, of course, but you already knew that. Then Rufus, on his old BSA, if it makes it. That piece of shit will probably end up in my truck for half of the trip. And you. I guess that's about it. It's not like the old days when we stretched out a mile down the highway."

"Well, folks don't want to make a commitment anymore," Mondo reflected. "Everyone seems to be in it for themselves. I guess we should feel lucky to have two prospects as lame as they are."

"Chow time!" Gypsy hollered from inside.

"Trust me. This will beat the hell out of prison food," I bragged. "Gypsy makes some amazing enchiladas."

"I can't wait!" Mondo was in the door ahead of me.

Gypsy really outdid herself with homemade salsa and pico de gallo. All through dinner she shot me these sexy little glances like I hadn't seen in years. I didn't know where that was coming from but I knew it would be a real sweet evening. After dinner we all kicked back on the front porch and knocked back a few longnecks. Gypsy rolled a big hooter and shared it with me. Mondo sipped his beer and we talked about the old days. The moon rose in the east. As midnight approached, Mondo excused himself and straddled his pristine Panhead. The open pipes shattered the silence as his taillight faded into the night. Gypsy hooked her thumb into my belt loop and slid her other arm around my neck. "Sweet evenin'," she yawned, plastering her wiry little body against me. Some days are better than others. It's a fortunate man who has a lover familiar with his every desire. I'm that man. My Gypsy put me in a place I rarely go and a wave of dreamless sleep overcame me.

*****

It's another story Wednesday night and I'm still having trouble with the LEDs blowing fuses. About 11pm I ripped them off the bike and threw them on the work bench. I had a beer and jumped in the shower. Gypsy's deep in slumber when I lay down beside her around midnight. Staring up at the ceiling fan, and staring, and waiting for sleep, I became more and more frustrated. The anticipation of the summer run was tinged with shades of dread. At some point, I finally dozed off. At 4am, I suddenly felt wide awake. In the dark house Gypsy stretched beside me breathing slowly. I slipped out of bed and made some coffee. As I drank the bitter brew, the expectation overwhelmed me. I'd saved myself a special treat. Without further hesitation I rinsed out my spoon and cup and refilled it halfway with tap water, dropped in the spoon and carried it out to my work bench. Once there, I dried the spoon on a paper towel, put a slight bend in the handle and sat it on the bench. From my toolbox I took a vial of course amber powder, a length of rubber vacuum line and a new syringe. I shook a generous amount of powder into the spoon. Then I drew up some water and dripped it into the spoon, dissolving the powder. I pulled the mixture into the syringe and took a deep breath. My hands were trembling slightly. I wrapped the vacuum line around my left bicep and held it tightly with my teeth. As I made a fist, a vein rose on my forearm. I pierced the vein with the needle and a whorl of blood rushed into the cylinder. As I released the tourniquet, I slowly pushed the plunger. A white hot iciness coursed through my body. The years peeled away and I felt young and strong again. I stashed the vial in my pocket.

Outside in the back yard every drop of dew sparkled on the grass. The cicadas screamed their songs and I could almost understand the words. With everything was in motion, I took a deep breath and felt the cool sweat on my temples. Behind me I heard the spring on the screen door popping as it stretched. I turned and Gypsy stood staring at me, moonlight flashing on the whites of her eyes. Her curly black hair floated on the warm summer breeze like angel's wings. Onyx lips broke the silence. "Early start?"

"I couldn't sleep. God, you are beautiful in the moonlight."

She almost smiled but sadness shrouded her like a soft burden. She turned and disappeared inside. I returned to my observation of the dawning day.

At eight o'clock it's time to begin preparations for the event. Gypsy backed the Chevy up to the garage and I began loading the coolers, grill, toolboxes and gas cans. Several of the guys show up early to help. Around nine, Shaggy pulled up on his old Goldwing, followed by Stella in her Tacoma, the bed stacked high with cases of canned beer. She jumped out of the cab clutching 2 fifths of Crown Royal.

"What do I hear for these puppies?" She held the bottles up to her ample breasts. "Bidding starts at twenty dollars, that's *each*, Boys." She laughed, handing me the "jugs" to place in the cooler. Roby, June and Bear transferred the rest of the bounty to my truck.

By 10, everybody arrived except Mondo and Rufus. Patty cracked open her fourth beer. She leaned against the back of my truck, attempting to contort her massive torso into a seductive pose. "Wolf, you're tweaking your ass off!" She slurs. "How about you hooking me and T-Bone up with a bump. I'll gladly make it worth your while when the sun goes down." She gives me a wink.

"I tell you what. I'll hook y'all up in a bit. We can meet in the garage. You can save that ample ass for your ole man. We'll just call this a favor." I laid a couple of thin lines out on the work bench. That ought to wake them up some.

In the distance I heard the rumble of Mondo's Panhead accompanied by what sounded like a lawnmower running on bad gas. Rufus and Mondo arrived together.

"I stopped by to help get his BSA dialed in," Mondo said. "I think it'll be okay if he fills it up with some premium." Mondo says little else. He seems reticent.

"Let's hit the road. We'll stop at the Texaco, gas up and buy ice, then hit 332 to Brazoria, up to West Columbia and out 35 south." I wanted to get the show on the road. "Patty, go tell Gypsy and Naomi to quit painting their nails and let's get our asses in gear!" I'm ready to ride! The sound of the engines starting ripped a jagged gash in the morning, spilling us out onto the highway. I took the lead with Bear to my right. The truck brought up the rear.

The fuel stop took longer than I'd hoped. Bear and Mondo seem a little irritable. Screw 'em. I paid for all the gas just to speed up the process. It didn't go over well with Gypsy. Screw her, too. We hit SH35 after noon and the Fourth of July traffic already sucked. With the temperature is in the mid nineties the heat radiated from the asphalt, making the southern headwind a blast furnace at these slow speeds. As we pulled into the city limits of Bay City, Mondo rolled up on my left and pointed at his tank, signaling another fuel stop. I nodded and he dropped back. Once on the main drag, I spotted a Shell truck stop with a large shaded parking area so I pulled ahead and glided into the pump area. Everyone congregated around one fuel island. I dismounted and proclaimed, "It's on y'all this time. I ain't paying."

As the Chevy pulled in, a rusty old K car chugged in behind. Out piled three vaguely familiar young girls wearing bikini tops, cutoffs and flip flops.

"I thought y'all would at least wait on us. Hell, we <u>are</u> the entertainment!" hollered the driver, removing her mirrored shades. I recognized them as some of the Houston girls who hung around Shaggy's in the summer. Tina and Wendy I knew. Another girl, a skinny kid that I immediately assumed to be jail bait, introduced herself as Sami. Wendy gravitated over to Roby, trying to negotiate a ride, telling him how much she likes the "feel" of a British bike. It worked.

As we prepared to leave, three Bay City patrol cars pulled into the parking lot, positioning their vehicles around us as to assert their sovereignty. Psycho stepped off his scooter. I intercepted him. "Let Bear handle this. It's his specialty." My word maked little difference. Fortunately, Naomi came up and ask him to help her load more ice into the coolers.

Apparently, Bear can tell who is in charge. It still amazes me how he does it but when we left we had a police escort through town and a friendly wave at the city limits. We're finally able to ride at a comfortable 60 miles per hour for a while.

As we approached Rockport, the traffic began to slow again. We made an uneventful fuel stop. The local economy, more accustomed to motorcycle clubs, knew we dropped money like peanut shells. With less than 100 miles to go and everyone was thirsty, I pulled over in a rest area south of Rockport. We hit the coolers hard, everyone slamming a couple of beers. Wendy, Tina and Sami made the rounds getting to know everyone. I snuck off to the perimeter with Gypsy and we both did a little bump from my vial.

"I'm tired of driving the truck," she told me. "I wish I was in the wind, like you!"

"Me too," I said." Why don't you let Naomi drive for a spell. I've got the wrong seat but one of the guys would be proud for you to ride with them."

"It's not the same. Besides, how would it look?"

"Who gives a shit. We know what's up!" I said.

"I'll let Naomi drive, but I'm going to stay with the truck," She reconciled. "We should go."

"Let everyone relax for a minute. We have a while."

"We don't want to set up in the dark."

"No, but it would be in our favor to hit the beach as it's cooling off." We stood together and watched the breeze tease the prairie grass as the wizard renewed our energy. Rowdy noises brought us around as the road called.

When we pulled out, Wendy drove the K car again and Tina planted herself on the back of Greg's rice burner, her eyes glazed and a big cannabis grin on her face. There would be no more stops until the beach. Anticipation was electric. The familiar edges of dusk caressed the western horizon as we found a secluded campsite at South Padre.

It's not as easy to maneuver a road bike in deep sand as one might think. A couple of the guys fishtailed, T-Bone made Patty dismount to walk and Rufus went down completely. Though he was uninjured, his BSA sparkled with the dusty sand. He threw a temper tantrum, kicking his bike and swearing to turn around and leave. Mondo got him back under control, righting his machine and agreeing to stay back with him and Patty as they slowly manipulated their way through the muck.

We set camp with the expertise of many weekends of experience. The prospects gathered driftwood for a fire. Beers were voraciously consumed as Gypsy, Patty and Naomi began grilling burgers. Sami offered to help and scored the barmaid gig.

"Keep their tongues wet!" Naomi chided her. "They're always happy when a sweet young thing keeps a cold one in their hand. Watch out, though, a couple of them may tend to get a little frisky." Something she soon experienced when Leland grabbed her butt and then pulled back his hand as if he had received a third degree burn. That was nothing compared to Jack demanding a wet kiss for his empty can.

"Only if it's really empty!" she said, taking the can and draining a few drops onto her pink tongue. "Nope, not good enough, try again." She laughed, handing him a fresh one.

Darkness fell hard as the sun set well before the moon rose. The blazing camp fire compelled our primal shadows to dance against the chrome and glossy steel of our iron horses.

Our appetites for food and beverage finally satiated, we moved on to more aboriginal desires. While pairings and groupings drifted away and a couple of the guys fired up their scooters to go in search of local talent, I sidled up to my Gypsy and suggested we take a swim in the surf. We walked down the beach until we were out of sight. We removed our clothes, wrapped them in a towel and ran into the waves, jumping the breakers in the darkness. We stopped at waist depth to press our salty bodies together and fall sideways into the surge.

*****

The guttural roar of V-twins roused the camp from sleep. When the sun was well into its daily arc Jack and Leland rode in. Their good fortunes and silver tongues found them other accommodations for the night. As I crawled into the brightness I saw T-Bone coaxing heat from the coals of the dormant camp fire, a charred aluminum coffee pot steaming in the debris. Patty was slumped on the tailgate of the truck drinking a beer.

"Breakfast of champions?" I asked. "Hell, not a bad idea. It is the weekend, unofficially."

Patty tossed me a can. As everyone dragged themselves into consciousness, many headed for the dunes. The less constrained of the group did little more than turn away to relieve their bladders.

"Lovely morning!" I exclaimed, holding my beer high with one hand while aiming my stream at the sand with the other.

"What's on the agenda for today?" Jack asked, clearly rested and ready.

"Ain't one," I said. "We rode in together. We'll ride out together on Sunday. This is home base. The rest is up to you. I'm not your daddy. You figure it out. As for me, I'm gonna drink beer and fish, maybe hit a couple of the local joints tonight if anybody's up for it."

Bruce and Rufus decided to join the fishing expedition. "We'll catch dinner," Rufus boasted optimistically.

Meanwhile Gypsy crawled out of our tent. "I'm going to Port Isabelle for supplies and check out the shops," She stated. "Naomi's riding along. We'll need the truck."

"Mind if I tag along?" Sami asked, her head sticking out of Mondo's tent, eyes squinting in the brightness. Gypsy and Naomi smiled at each other. They'd taken a liking to the feisty kid.

"Sure, if you can pull yourself loose from that old jailbird," Naomi said.

I'm thinking, *"What do you use to catch a jailbird? Jail bait, of course,"* but I didn't say it. Mondo still snored.

"Y'all drop us at the pier on your way and be back to pick us up later," I told Gypsy,

"well before dark." We unloaded all but one cooler and the fishing gear. Bruce, Rufus and I piled in the back. We headed for the pier as everyone else made plans for the day. The pier we stopped at had a bar and grill with a bait shop. I could live there for a week.

Fishing slowed the day but not to the point of boredom. We landed a few specks, some drum, one flounder and a nice sized snook. Rufus hooked a hammerhead that must have been close to 4 feet long but after fighting for a good 20 minutes it broke free. "Damn!"

Well into the afternoon Jack and Leland pulled up on their bikes, waving frantically and revving the engines. I walked up to the shoreline where Jack dismounted and paced franticly.

"Psycho got busted!" He yelled when I was in earshot.

"I'll be right down." As I went back to get my tackle, Bruce and Rufus reeled in, seeing the signs of stress.

"What's up?" Rufus asked.

"Cops got Psycho! Y'all can stay if you want but I need to see what I can do."

"Bro, we're in this together," Bruce said and we packed up our gear.

"So what happened?" I asked when we climbed down to the beach.

"Psycho got stupid," Jack stated.

"Hey! He was just being Psycho," Leland retorted. "That asshole didn't have to challenge him."

Anyway, the gist of the situation was my three buddies cruising the south beach where all the college kids were hanging, checking out the tail. Whenever they got thirsty they found a group of kids and took some beer. Usually the kids shared, sometimes even inviting them to party along. This tactic usually worked for Psycho but he picked the wrong kids this time.

"So, you guys want to give up a few beers for some thirsty bikers?" Psycho asked, strutting up to a small group with Jack and Leland flanking him.

"Not today, son!" Some skinhead body builder type decided to show off for his little blonde girlfriend. "It would be best if y'all just moved your skanky asses down the beach."

"I tell you what, Studly, I'll move my skanky ass down the beach right after you provide me and my buddies with an ample supply of cervesa! I might even take your little blonde bitch along and show her a real party!" That's Psycho. Just as the big cowboy began to take a swing, Psycho pulled a 9mm Glock from his waist band and stuck it in Studly's face.

"Beer! Now!" Psycho screamed. Hey, bitch, grab a couple of six packs and hand them to my bros before I give your meat sack here a third eye socket. Make it quick, my hands get shaky when I'm thirsty! Be sweet about it. Hell, give 'em a big sloppy kiss while you're at it so's Mr. Studly can see how to appreciate such fine tail." She responded, though honestly she didn't put her best effort into the kiss. Then she skittered over to hide behind Studly.

"Thanks for your generosity," Psycho smiled. "Y'all just sit tight until we leave and then you can resume your lame ass festivities.

Last chance to ride with a real man, sweetie. No? Shame then. Y'all have fun!"

"So," as Leland said, "that should have been the end of it." However, within twenty minutes the three "outlaws" were surrounded by 6 county cop cars containing very unhappy deputies with 12 gauge shotguns. As it turned out the cowboy only wanted to press charges on Psycho. He'll most likely be charged with armed robbery and God knows what he'll get for the kissing thing. So Psycho is in the Cameron County jail. The cops took his gun and impounded his bike. What are we going to do now?" Leland directed the question at me.

"That idiot could fuck up a wet dream!" I thought. "There ain't much we can do until he sees the judge and gets his bond set," is what I said. "Let's go back to camp. We can figure it out from there." I rode back with Leland and sent Tina back for Bruce and Rufus. Then I sent T-Bone and Patty to Port Isabelle to try and round up the girls. I figured Naomi wanted to know what's up with Psycho. That all done, I crawled in my tent and took a hefty bump from my vial. I needed to think.

We didn't have an attorney but we did have a bail bondsman we worked with back home. Bear kept his number but Bear wasn't around. I sent Jack and Leland to find him. They'd seen him earlier hanging with Mondo at a local watering hole. So much for fishing, or anything else anytime soon! Shit!

As everybody began showing back up, camp resembled a fire ant mound that suffered a stampede, with everyone edgy and pissed. My job entailed getting them settled down and focused on the situation at hand, like herding cats.

I decided that Bear, Mondo and I would ride into Brownsville and try to spring Psycho. Bruce rode along since he had access to money.

By the time we reached the county jail Psycho was charged with aggravated assault with a deadly weapon and his bond set at $50.000.00, meaning we would have to come up with at least $5,000.00 to free him. Our bondsman referred us to a local guy who could bond him out for $7,000.00. Bruce agreed to loan Psycho the money but wanted to meet with him first to set up the deal. Unfortunately, after hours visitation was only available accompanied by an attorney or bondsman. The bondsman, a skinny little shit in a crappy leisure suit, finally showed up half drunk after 10:30 at night. It took another hour and a half to get the paperwork done and free Psycho. By then, the bars were closed and Psycho was as nervous as a whore in church, making it a long ride back to South Padre.

We pulled into camp to find most of the group still up drinking beer around a roaring campfire. The story had morphed into the biggest heist in Cameron County history, with Psycho greeted like a conquering hero. I just shook my head and wandered off into the dunes for some peace and quiet. The stars looked down on me and I felt them laughing at my folly. I knew I should be back partying with the gang I had to clear my head. I sat there over an hour watching hermit crabs and lighting bugs, trying to formulate a question to ask myself. When I finally gave up and returned to camp I was eyed with a measure of unspoken suspicion. Maybe it was just me. I opened a beer, sat on a log and stared into the flames. No one, not even Gypsy, came over to converse. The night slowed to a crawl. The party wound down and I still sat on the log drinking beer when the dawn broke on the eastern horizon. I crawled into my tent. Gypsy was not there. I needed to doze for a few minutes then I could work it out, whatever it was.

I was simmering in a pool of my own sweat when I startled awake to the sound of a mass metal exodus. I stuck my head out into the searing sunlight and only Mondo and Bear remained. My truck was parked out by the water leaving only our three bikes at camp. I retreated back into the tent long enough to snort a capful of powder from my vial then walked into the dunes and took a long slow piss. As I returned to the embers of the previous night's fire, Mondo handed me a beer.

"Where's Gypsy?" I asked.

"Not sure," Bear grunted, "Not my problem." Our aura of camaraderie missing, silence reigned as my senses bristled.

Mondo spoke first. "Bro," a long pause, "we go way back, right?"

"Yeah." Come on, drop the other shoe.

"Some of the guys, myself included, think it might be time for an election, maybe a change in leadership"

"Well, I don't!" I exclaimed. "Maybe you should ask Bear how well that worked out for him. Screw you both!"

"Listen, Bro, I ain't trying to start any shit. It just seems like your losing focus and maybe you need a break from the pressure."

"Face it," Bear interrupted, "your strung out and fried. You need a long vacation."

"Fuck you! This is what I do! It's who I am! I've held this club together through some rough bullshit and now you want to toss me out?! Good luck on that! I'll take out the first motherfucker that tries it!"

"Honestly, we would rather not do it that way. How about an open election, not today, we can set it up when we get back to Freeport. No rush. Keep it civilized." Mondo, always the diplomat, trying his persuasive tactics.

"Kiss my ass!" I replied. "Give me another beer!"

Mondo obliged.

"Where the fuck is my ole lady?" I was getting peeved. "This is bullshit!"

"She didn't want to be here for this," Mondo explained. "She took off with the others. I think she might be scared of your reaction."

"That's a bunch of crap. That little bitch ain't scared of shit! What did you tell her?"

"Seriously," Mondo was trying to smooth the ruffled feathers, "why don't you just think about it? We're not trying to get rid of you. We just think you need some time to regroup."

"So this is some kind of intervention? Why don't we just change our name to the Touchy-Feely Motorcycle Club? You guys are fucking idiots!"

Bear stepped up. "Fine! It's gonna happen! Deal with it or not! It would damn sure be in your best interest to work with us."

I straddled my bike and fired it up, pulling away, dramatically showering the entire camp with a sheet of sand.

I had to find Gypsy. I rode up and down the beach. I cruised the coastal highway. I went in to Port Isabelle. No Gypsy. I didn't see any of the gang. I did run in to Tina and Wendy at a convenience store on the coastal highway. They didn't know where she was except she was last seen riding with June as the group headed up north.

The girls were glad to see me. They asked if I would like to go to the south beach with them and hang out.

"Did y'all ditch Sami?" I asked.

"She's with the bikes. I think she's riding with Greg. She's a real pothead at heart," Wendy giggled. "Me, I'm more a fan of nose candy."

I couldn't really think of anywhere north to look for the group so I figured I would take the path of least resistance. "It's quite possible I could help you with that. Why don't you ladies join me in the john?"

"Kinky!" Tina said. "I like!"

I was only about half way through the eight ball I had started with so I laid out three fat lines on top of the toilet tank. "Ladies first." As they each bent over to snort their lines, I gently slid my hand up their inner thigh to the top of their tight blue jean cutoffs. Wendy pretended not to notice but Tina wiggled provocatively and thrust her ass firmly into my hand. When I bent down to do my line, it wasn't there. Both girls smiled demurely so I set out two more and did them both myself.

"Let's go get wet," Tina said, slipping her hand under my t-shirt. "I'll ride with you." Wendy followed in the car back to the south beach. Tina had to share my butt bucket on the way, forcing her to press her puerile body firmly against my back while her tiny hands found their mark below my navel where the seat met my thighs. Due to her gentle massage, I was fully erect when we hit the beach road. It was next to impossible to find a deserted stretch of beach on the gulf side but after following the frontage north for a way, the crowd thinned out. I pulled my bike back into the dunes while Wendy parked just off the road, blocking the entrance to our private hideaway. Tina ran over and popped open the trunk, dragging out a couple of blankets and a small ice chest.

"Good place to get a tan." Wendy removed her bikini top exposing her lightly freckled breasts and seductively slathered them with coconut oil. "Want to do my back?" She asked. She'd obviously loosened up.

 Hey, save some for me!" Tina yelled, after laying out the blankets.

"He's a big guy," Wendy said. "I think there's enough of him for both of us. We're just two little girls, after all."

"I think she meant the lotion," I said.

"Not really!" Tina giggled, removing her clothes and stretching out on the blanket.

"Didn't you ladies want to get wet?" I asked.

"I don't know about Tina, but I'm pretty wet already," Wendy said, tossing Tina the lotion.

"Come lube me up, Wolf," Tina said. While I oiled every square inch of her body, Wendy drenched almost all of my body.

"Ain't you forgetting something?" I asked her, looking down at my erection.

"This stuff doesn't taste as good as it smells," Wendy said. "I know what boys like!"

Tina whispered to me loud enough for Wendy to hear. "I know what *men* like!" She grabbed Wendy's hand and pulled her down on top, kissing her deeply. Tina writhed under Wendy, her small pale breasts slipping against Wendy's ample freckled orbs. I reached over and slid two fingers into Wendy and pressed my thumb firmly against her anus. As she whimpered, Tina pulled me down beside them and sandwiched Wendy between us.

By the time the bottle of lotion was gone, I was just as empty. The girls were still feeling frisky and ran off to play in the surf. I lay back and, though not sleepy, closed my eyes to bask in the afterglow. I had been slipping in and out of dreamland for some time when the sound of a familiar engine stopped nearby. I opened my eyes and spied my old Chevy parked behind the K car. Gypsy was leaning against the front fender, her arms crossed in front of her.

"Hey, baby, I've been looking for you," I stammered, grabbing for my pants.

"I see that," She said, her eyes surveying the scene. "I'm going back to camp."

"I'm right behind you."

"It doesn't matter, you do what you want."

I figured she didn't really mean that the way I hoped she did. She started the truck and pulled away, not looking back.

Tina and Wendy came strolling hand in hand across the beachfront. Rivulets of seawater were sliding down their oily bodies, leaving little wet spots on the sand.

"Hey, Wolf. Who was that?" Tina asked.

"Gypsy."

"Oh, shit! Are you in trouble?"

"Nothing I can't handle," I said, trying to convince myself. "I should probably go back and patch it up though."

"Can we get another little bump before you go?" Wendy asked.

"Sure, why not." I dressed and pulled out my vial. It was on the downhill side of half full. I laid out three lines on a suitcase in the car. "You girls go ahead but save one for me this time." We did our lines and each of them gave me a full body kiss. "I had a blast," I told them. They smiled at each other.

"Maybe we can do it again sometime." Tina touched my face. They turned and trotted back toward the water. I started my bike and headed back toward camp. As I arrived, the big orange sun was almost ready to slip behind the dunes. A party was in full swing. Bear had a couple of briskets on the grill, a large camp fire was blazing and Lynard Skynard was blasting from the truck's powerful stereo.

There seemed to be a noticeable shift in mood as I stepped off my bike. "Let's rock and roll!" I yelled and things almost went back to normal party mode. I didn't immediately see Gypsy so I walked over to check out the grill and get a beer.

"Done any thinking about our conversation?" Bear asked.

"Yeah, we can talk when we get home," I said. I had no intention of rolling over but I didn't think it was a good time to force a confrontation.

"Works for me," he replied and stabbed a fork deep into the brisket, flipping it with a popping sizzle. I stood a minute. Nothing more was said so I went looking for Gypsy. I found her out in the dunes smoking a joint with Naomi, Patty, T-Bone, Sami and Greg. The conversation died as I walked up.

"Hey, Wolf," Greg said, "get a hit of this new Guatemalan shit I've got. It'll smooth you out."

"He ain't bullshitting," T-Bone agreed. "It's takin' all three of my legs just to stand up!" Patty and Sami laughed so hard I was afraid their faces might explode. I took a long deep toke and passed it to Gypsy.

"Sorry about today, baby," I apologized.

"It don't matter, Roman, you're who you are, you do what you do. It's always been that way. I don't suppose anything will change."

"I reckon not," I allowed.

"Awk—ward!" Patty belched.

"Hey, y'all, it's a party! Lighten up," Sami squealed, still giggling.

"Yeah, we're cool," Gypsy said. "Right, Wolf?"

"Yeah, Baby, sure." I hoped it was true but she hadn't put much heart into it. We finished the joint and wandered back to the party. As the sun slipped below the horizon, the party was revving up. Beer was flowing. The brisket was excellent. Psycho was reveling in his fifteen minutes of fame, the story growing increasingly bizarre. Almost all the food was gone when Tina and Wendy showed up with 2 quart bottles of Jack Daniels and began passing them around. The fog settled in well before midnight. As it rolled in, it wiped out my memory. I can vaguely remember the dreams of the bats. The furry little creatures attaching themselves to my neck, face and groin. I'm paralyzed. I can only lay in horror as they slowly reduce me to an empty shell while squeaking their demonic little giggles. I start awake. The tent is stifling. The sun is up. I am alone.

*****

I force myself to reconnect with conscious thought and the sound of voices outside. I need to get it together. I look around, a couple of beer cans, all my clothes, some other clothes I don't recognize. Girl stuff. Not Gypsy's. Shit, this ain't good! I grab my pants and check the pockets for my vial. It's there, but almost empty. I snort the contents then pour in a few drops of beer from one of the empty cans and drink the residual. I manage to swallow the resulting vomit. Nothing lost. My head is clearing. It's time to make my entrance. I dress. Emerging into the searing sunlight I notice the fog has lifted. The gang is experiencing a communal hangover. Everyone moves slowly as if dancing to a dirge. Several bodies are still passed out in the sand. T-Bone, Patty and some guy I don't recognize are sitting on a log staring into the dying embers of last evening's fire. Mondo sits on the tailgate of the Chevy, Sami's head in his lap. Her delicate snore is rhythmically pacing the slow dance of those waking souls trying desperately to prepare for the day. I walk to the door of the Chevy. Gypsy is stretched out on the seat, sleeping peacefully, her jeans on the floorboard, her black thong underwear hanging on the shifter. My mind can't process that right now. I check the coolers, there are scant few cans left. I grab one, pop it open and take a walk toward the surf. Though my memory is vague, my mind is clearing. It doesn't help with my convoluted situation.

The morning is cool for July, a brisk breeze blowing off the Gulf. It only takes a short walk to realize that I need to regain control. Walking briskly back to camp, I announce my intention to be on the road in one hour. "It's a long drive back to Freeport. Traffic will be heavy. Everyone needs to pack up." Although a few grumbles are heard, the group begins breaking camp. Soon we're ready to head out.

Wendy and Tina apparently left before dawn, leaving Sami to ride back with us. Gypsy's alone, driving the truck while Naomi rides with Psycho. We head toward Port O'Conner and I pull in at the same store where I ran in to Wendy and Tina the day before. We pull up at the two gas pumps for a fill up. Toward the back of the line I hear the words "arrogant asshole" from Naomi and she stomps over to the truck, getting in the passenger side and slamming the door.

Patty stomps out of the store. "Too early to buy beer," she fumes and digs around in the cooler. She finds a couple of cans, chugs one and stuffs the other down the front of her pants. The attendant comes out and tells her she can't drink on the premises.

"Fuck you!" she screams. "Who made you fuckin' king?" T-Bone gets off his bike and struts toward the building. The attendant runs back inside and locks the door. Power goes out at the pumps.

"Screw him!" I say. He doesn't want our business. We'll take it down the road." We mount up and pull away. As we do, everyone gives him the single finger salute. On down the coastal highway we find a truck stop and fuel up.

Gypsy is sitting at the fuel island in the Chevy so I go over to gas it up. "How're you doing, baby?" I asked her, smiling.

"Tired," she stares straight ahead.

"You want anything from the store?"

"Nope."

"How about a breakfast taco?"

"I'm good."

It doesn't seem like I'm going to get much out of her right now. "You okay?" I asked. She slowly turns her face toward me. Her eyes are smoldering, her features stony. By the red in her eyes I would have thought she had been crying if I didn't know her better. She exhales loudly and looks away.

"Just the gas," she states. I comply. Naomi looks at me out of the corner of her eye with an expression that could be anger, pity or disgust. It's hard to say.

The fueling done, I lead the way back out on the road. We haven't made 10 miles when Bear rides up beside me pointing behind us. A quarter mile back, several of the guys have pulled over. They're gathered around Rufus' BSA. A wisp of black smoke rises from under the seat.

"Electrical fire," he says when I get back to the scene. We unload the truck bed. Four of us lift the dead motorcycle into the truck and restack the supplies around it. Rufus climbs in the truck bed amongst the provisions, finds a renegade beer, pops it open and proceeds to make himself as comfortable as possible.

"Let's head out!" I once again lead the clan back out on the highway.

The traffic is moderate and the road hypnotic. Miles slowly peel away. To avoid the Corpus Christi bottleneck, I take 77 to Refugio. Just as I take the right on 774 to rejoin the coastal highway, Mondo and Bear blow past me signaling the group to follow them. By the time I get turned around I'm behind everyone. As I catch up to the truck I see that Rufus is no longer in the back. He's in the passenger seat with Naomi driving. I don't see Gypsy. The pace has picked up and we are cruising briskly along 77. I pull up beside the truck and motion to Rufus who just shrugs his shoulders and points ahead.

"Those Bastards! Who do they think they are. This is a bunch of shit! They can't just change the route without checking with me first. I'm gonna shut these fuckers down and kick some ass!"

I see a slight break in the oncoming traffic and I give her full throttle. The machine jumps to life. I fly past the group, open pipes screaming. As I pass, they startle and shift quickly to the right until I'm behind Mondo with Bear to his right, but Mondo is not giving way. He hugs the line. There's Gypsy, straddling his Panhead. I hit my clutch and gun the engine. Gypsy looks back and Mondo tries to wave me in behind.

"Fuck that!" I try to pass on the line but Mondo holds it tighter. Bear drops back slightly to keep me from going between them.

"Goddamn it!"

Gypsy turns and looks at me again, a dangerously defiant look. She presses herself firmly against Mondo, her slender arms encircling him. She turns her face away as her hands slide below his belt buckle.

"That fucking little bitch, I should have seen this coming!"

I see a break in the traffic. I pull up beside and gun my motor. Gypsy looks over. Mondo holds his ground.

"Fuckin' whore!" I scream. She released his groin just long enough to flip me off. Mondo frantically motions me to fall back. I do, just in time to avoid colliding with the first of three gravel trucks. The second one passes. I gun my engine and pull up beside Mondo. I raise the middle finger of my left hand high in the air.

"Fuck you all!" I scream and lean slightly to the left, grinning. Just before impact, I note the look of horror on the truck driver's face.

THE END

Acknowledgements

Bait first appeared in *Tidal Basin Review* Summer 2011

Fat Tuesday first appeared in *Fringe* Fall 2011

Life Amended first appeared in *Connotation Press* March 2012

Coyote was runner-up for the Mighty River Prize in 2011

Painting Over Stains first appeared in *Sixfold* Fall 2013

Willow Garden first appeared in *Frontier Tales #29*

Farm Work first appeared in *Harvest Time* (Inwood Indiana Press-2012)

The Bridge first appeared in *Fiction 365* December 2011

Vanishing Point first appeared in *Red Dirt Review* February 2012

Heat Lightning first appeared in *Short Story America Vol. III*

www.ingramcontent.com/pod-product-compliance
Lightning Source LLC
Chambersburg PA
CBHW022145240626
47153CB00007B/2512